RISE OF THE
TEENAGE MUTANT NINJA
TURTLES
SOUND OFF!

™

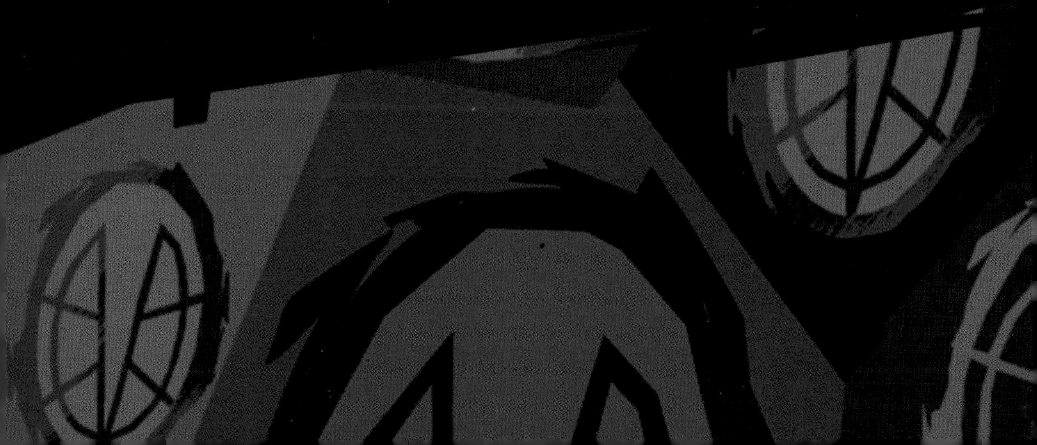

Become our fan on Facebook facebook.com/idwpublishing
Follow us on Twitter @idwpublishing
Subscribe to us on YouTube youtube.com/idwpublishing
See what's new on Tumblr tumblr.idwpublishing.com
Check us out on Instagram instagram.com/idwpublishing

Jerry Bennington, President
Nachie Marsham, Publisher
Cara Morrison, Chief Financial Officer
Matthew Ruzicka, Chief Accounting Officer
Rebekah Cahalin, EVP of Operations
John Barber, Editor-in-Chief
Justin Eisinger, Editorial Director, Graphic Novels and Collections
Scott Dunbier, Director, Special Projects
Blake Kobashigawa, VP of Sales
Lorelei Bunjes, VP of Technology & Information Services
Anna Morrow, Sr Marketing Director
Tara McCrillis, Director of Design & Production
Mike Ford, Director of Operations
Shauna Monteforte, Sr. Director of Manufacturing Operations

Ted Adams and Robbie Robbins, IDW Founders

Collection Edits
JUSTIN EISINGER
and ALONZO SIMON

Series Assistant Edits
MEGAN BROWN

Series Edits
BOBBY CURNOW

Collection Design
CHRISTA MIESNER

Cover Art
CHAD THOMAS

ISBN: 978-1-68405-616-3   23 22 21 20   2 3 4 5

Special thanks Joan Hilty and Linda Lee for their invaluable assistance.

For international rights, contact licensing@idwpublishing.com

WRITTEN BY

MATTHEW K. MANNING

ART BY

CHAD THOMAS

COLORS BY

HEATHER BRECKEL

LETTERS BY

CHRISTA MIESNER

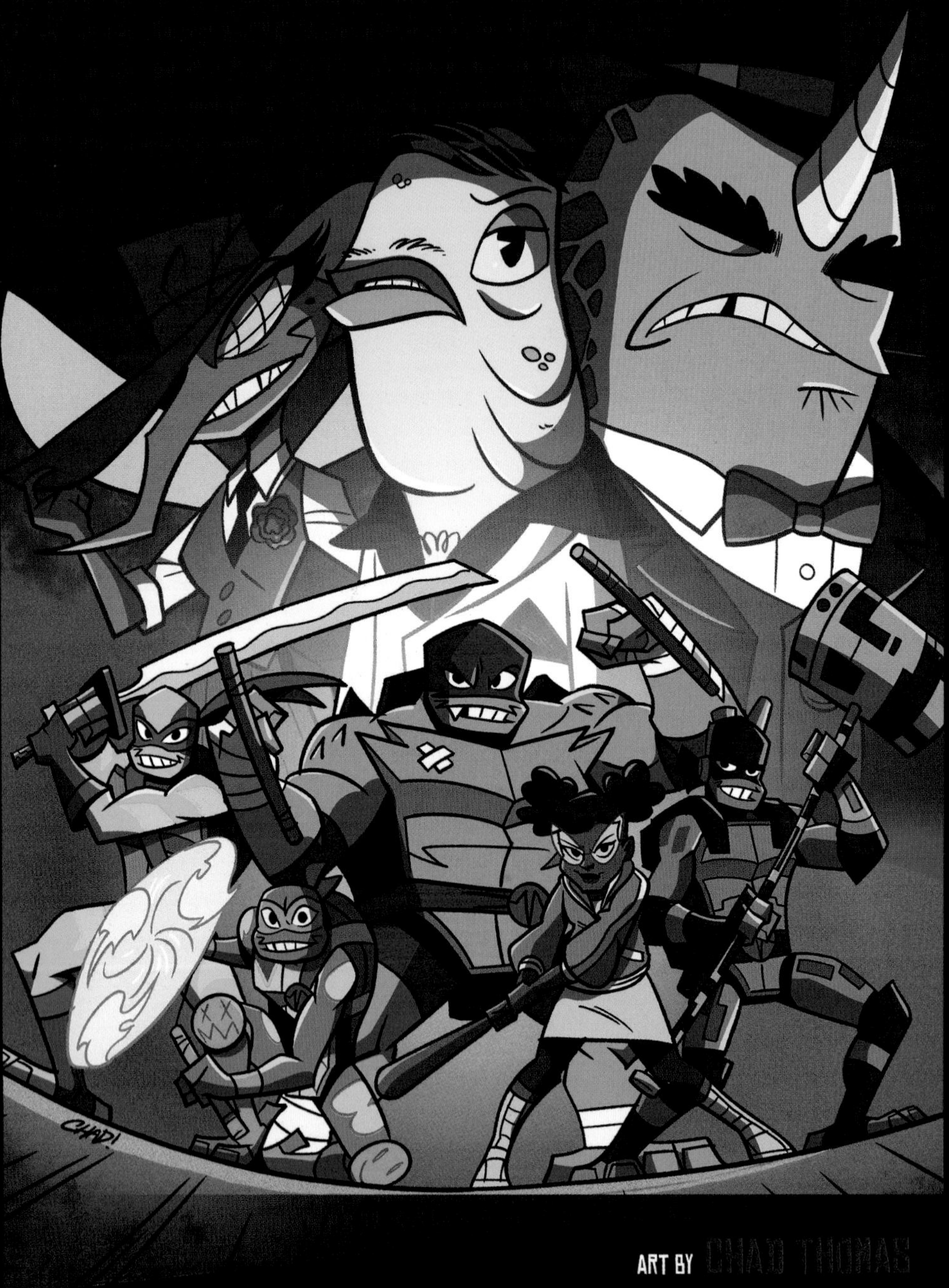
CHAD!

ART BY CHAD THOMAS

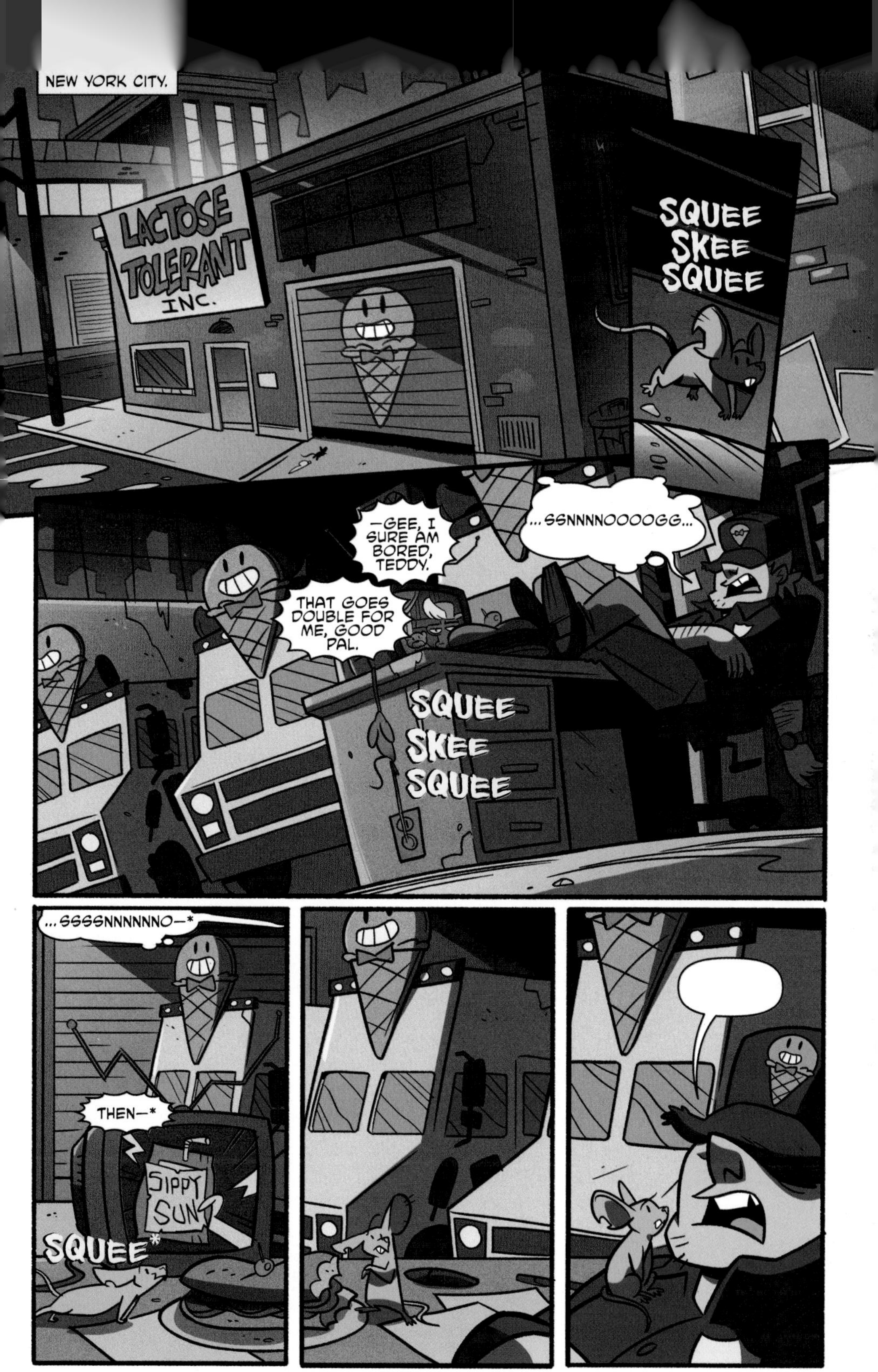
NEW YORK CITY.
LACTOSE TOLERANT INC.
SQUEE SKEE SQUEE
—GEE, I SURE AM BORED, TEDDY.
...SSNNNNOOOOGG...
THAT GOES DOUBLE FOR ME, GOOD PAL.
SQUEE SKEE SQUEE
...SSSSNNNNNNO—*
THEN—*
SIPPY SUN
SQUEE*

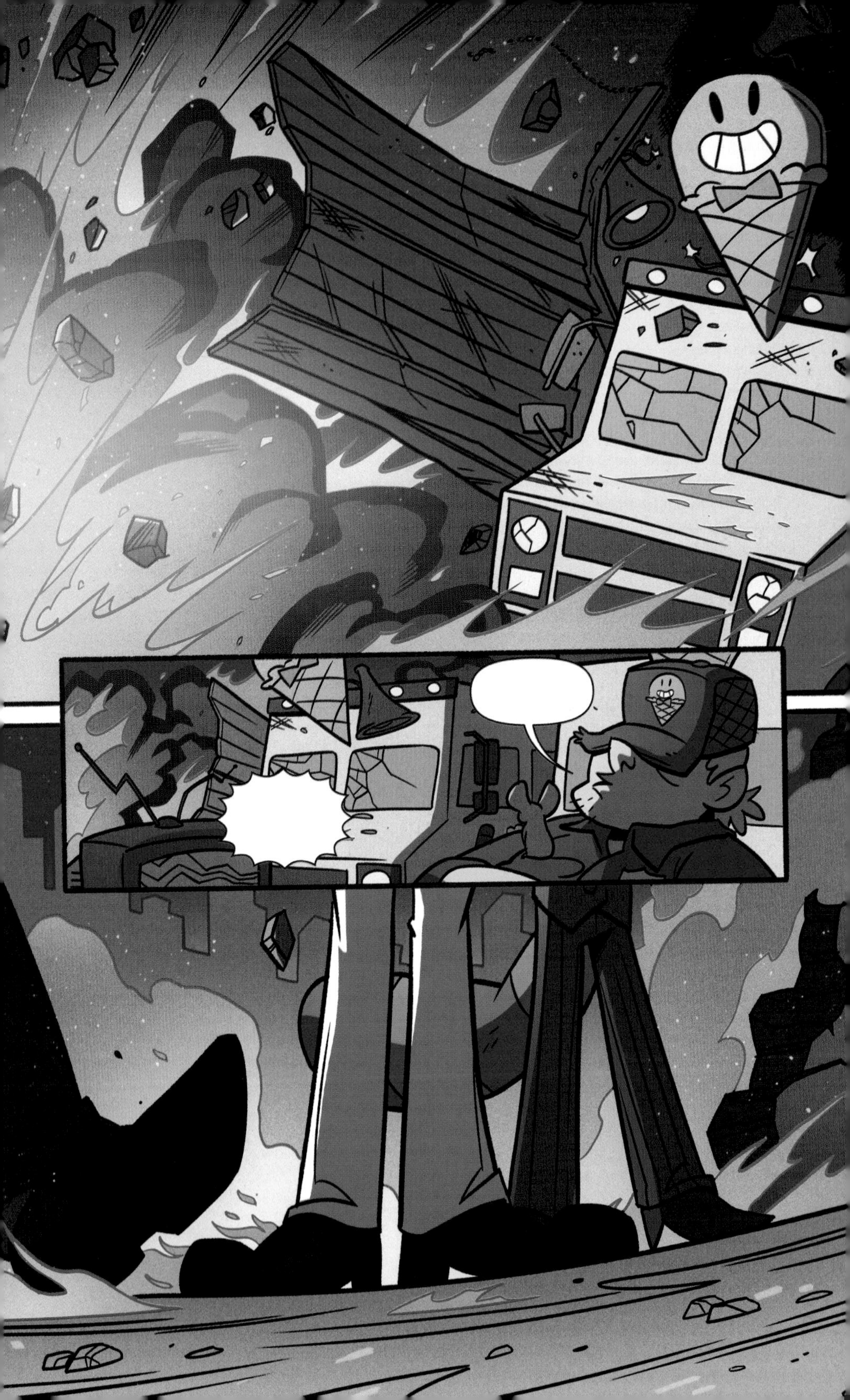

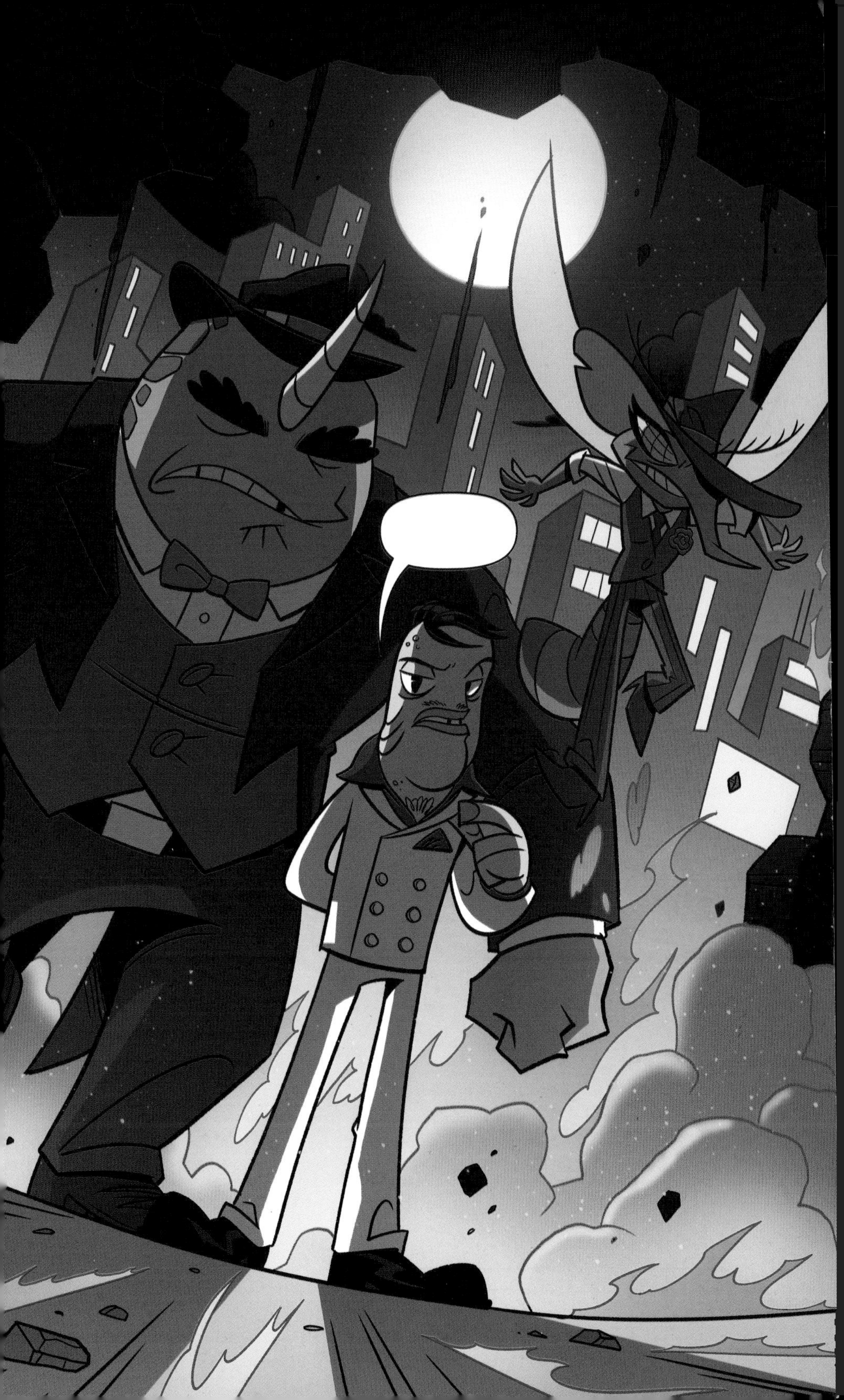

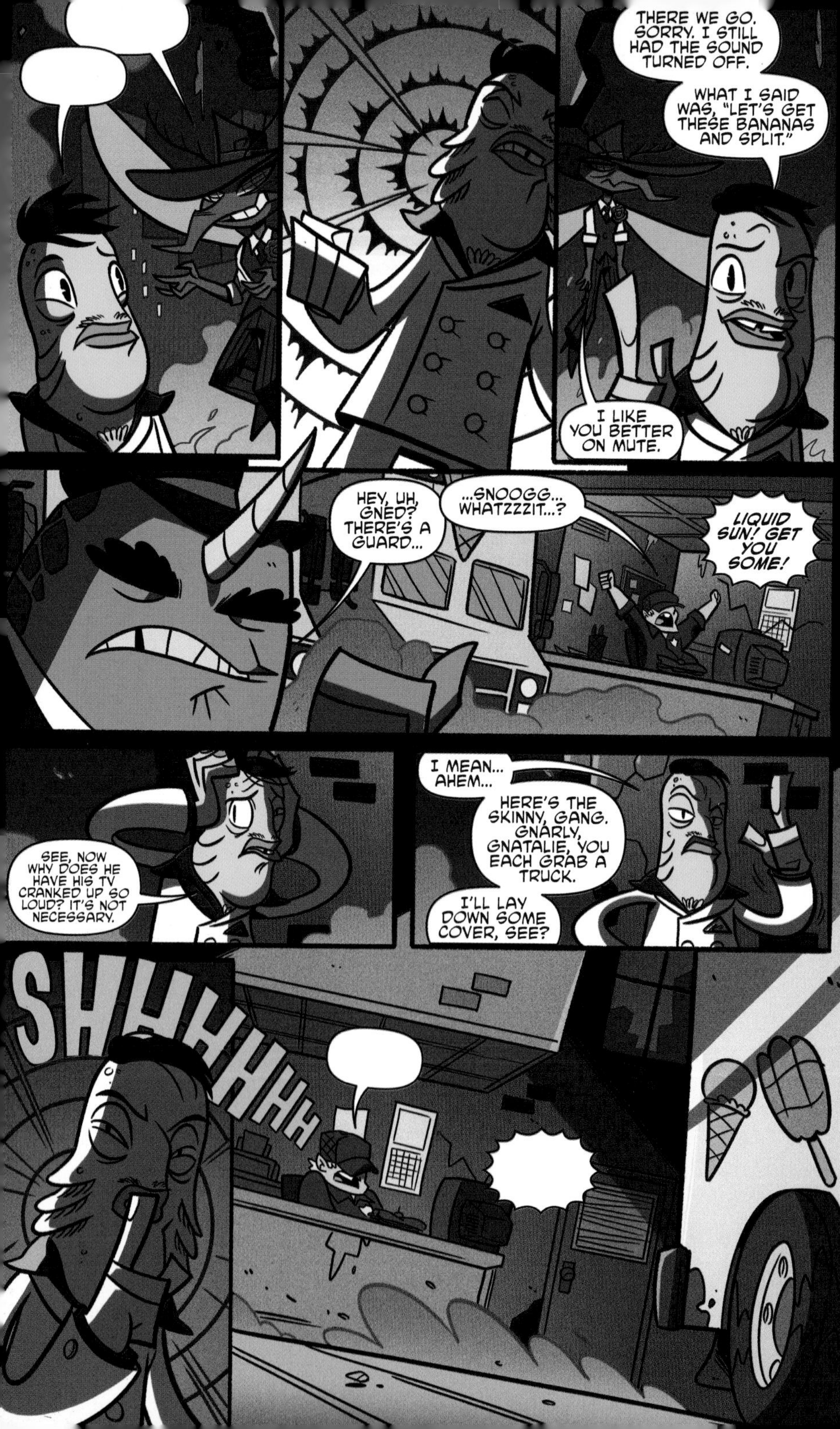
THERE WE GO. SORRY. I STILL HAD THE SOUND TURNED OFF.
WHAT I SAID WAS, "LET'S GET THESE BANANAS AND SPLIT."
I LIKE YOU BETTER ON MUTE.
HEY, UH, GNED? THERE'S A GUARD...
...SNOOGG... WHATZZZIT...?
LIQUID SUN! GET YOU SOME!
SEE, NOW WHY DOES HE HAVE HIS TV CRANKED UP SO LOUD? IT'S NOT NECESSARY.
I MEAN... AHEM...
HERE'S THE SKINNY, GANG. GNARLY, GNATALIE, YOU EACH GRAB A TRUCK.
I'LL LAY DOWN SOME COVER, SEE?
SHHHHHH

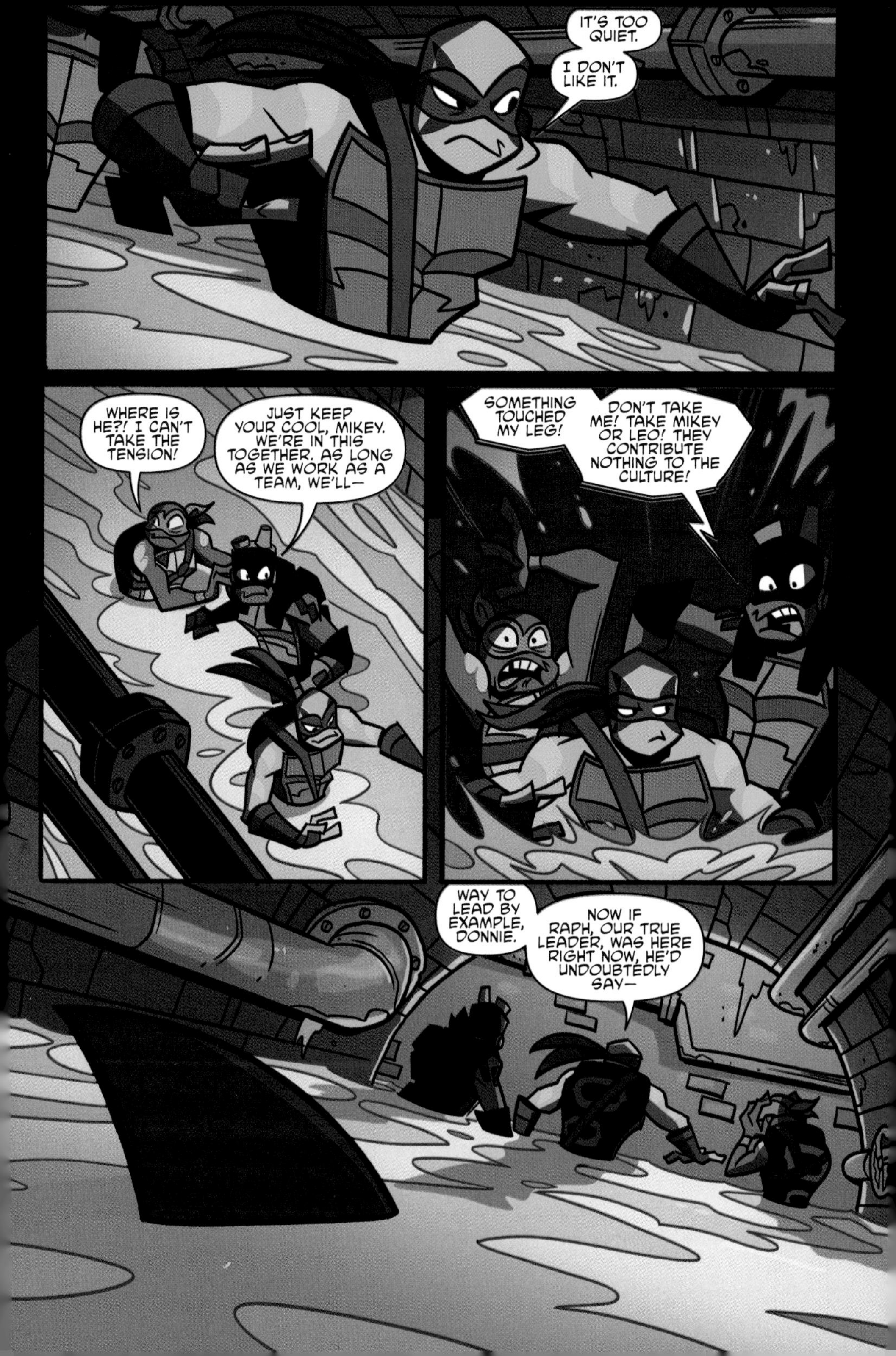
IT'S TOO QUIET.
I DON'T LIKE IT.
WHERE IS HE?! I CAN'T TAKE THE TENSION!
JUST KEEP YOUR COOL, MIKEY. WE'RE IN THIS TOGETHER. AS LONG AS WE WORK AS A TEAM, WE'LL—
SOMETHING TOUCHED MY LEG!
DON'T TAKE ME! TAKE MIKEY OR LEO! THEY CONTRIBUTE NOTHING TO THE CULTURE!
WAY TO LEAD BY EXAMPLE, DONNIE.
NOW IF RAPH, OUR TRUE LEADER, WAS HERE RIGHT NOW, HE'D UNDOUBTEDLY SAY—

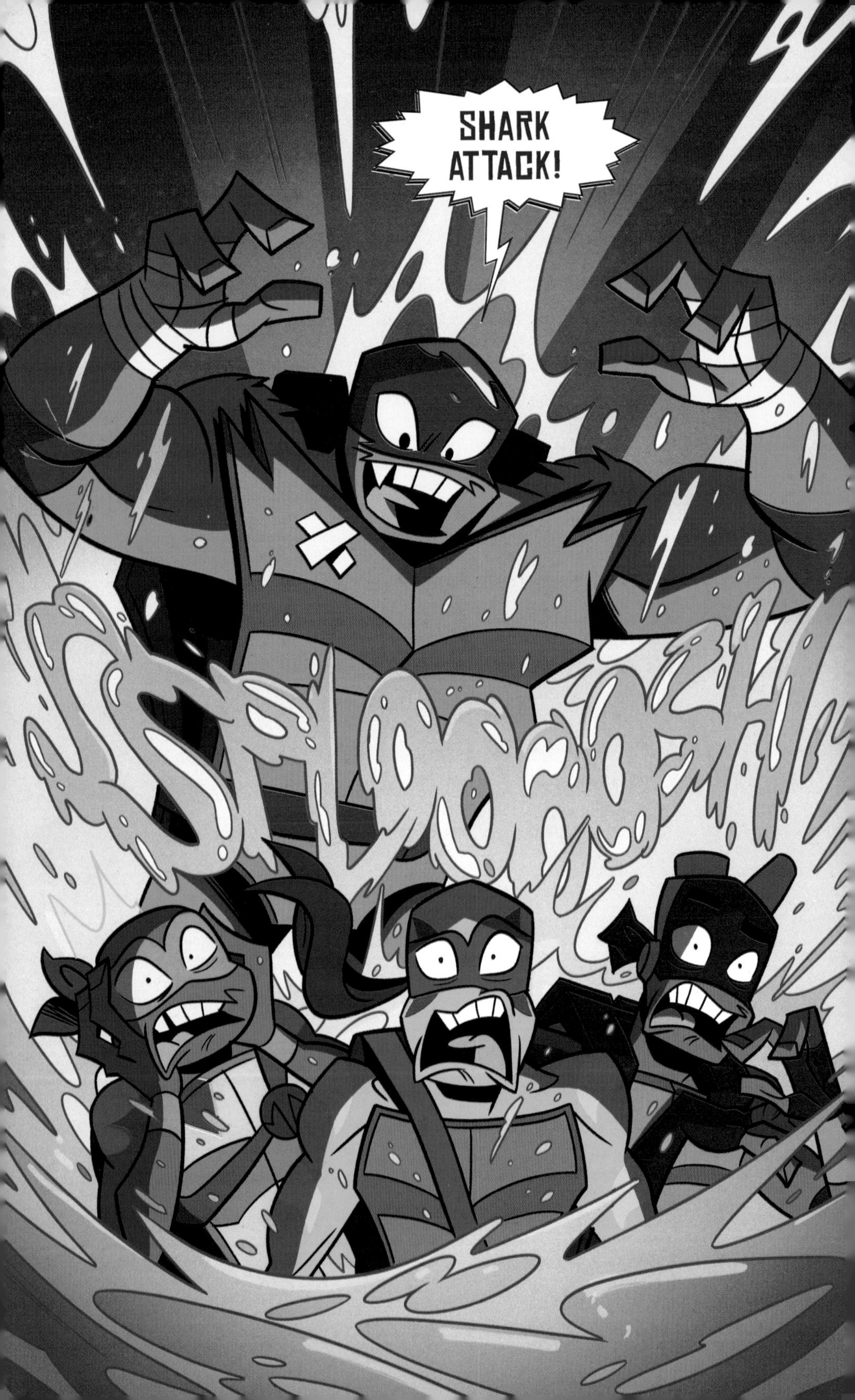
SHARK ATTACK!

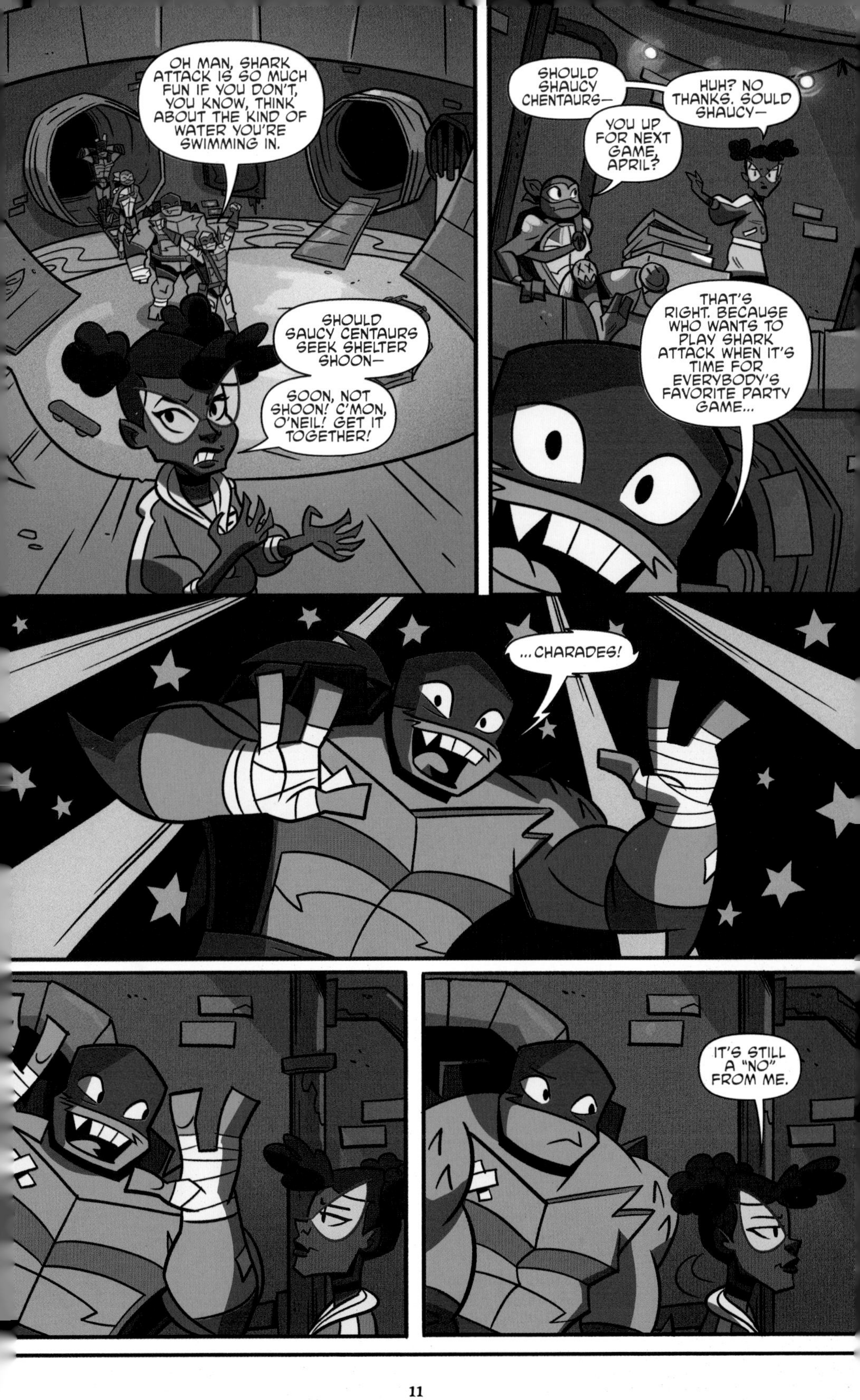
OH MAN, SHARK ATTACK IS SO MUCH FUN IF YOU DON'T, YOU KNOW, THINK ABOUT THE KIND OF WATER YOU'RE SWIMMING IN.
SHOULD SAUCY CENTAURS SEEK SHELTER SHOON—
SOON, NOT SHOON! C'MON, O'NEIL! GET IT TOGETHER!
SHOULD SHAUCY CHENTAURS—
YOU UP FOR NEXT GAME, APRIL?
HUH? NO THANKS. SOULD SHAUCY—
THAT'S RIGHT. BECAUSE WHO WANTS TO PLAY SHARK ATTACK WHEN IT'S TIME FOR EVERYBODY'S FAVORITE PARTY GAME...
...CHARADES!
IT'S STILL A "NO" FROM ME.

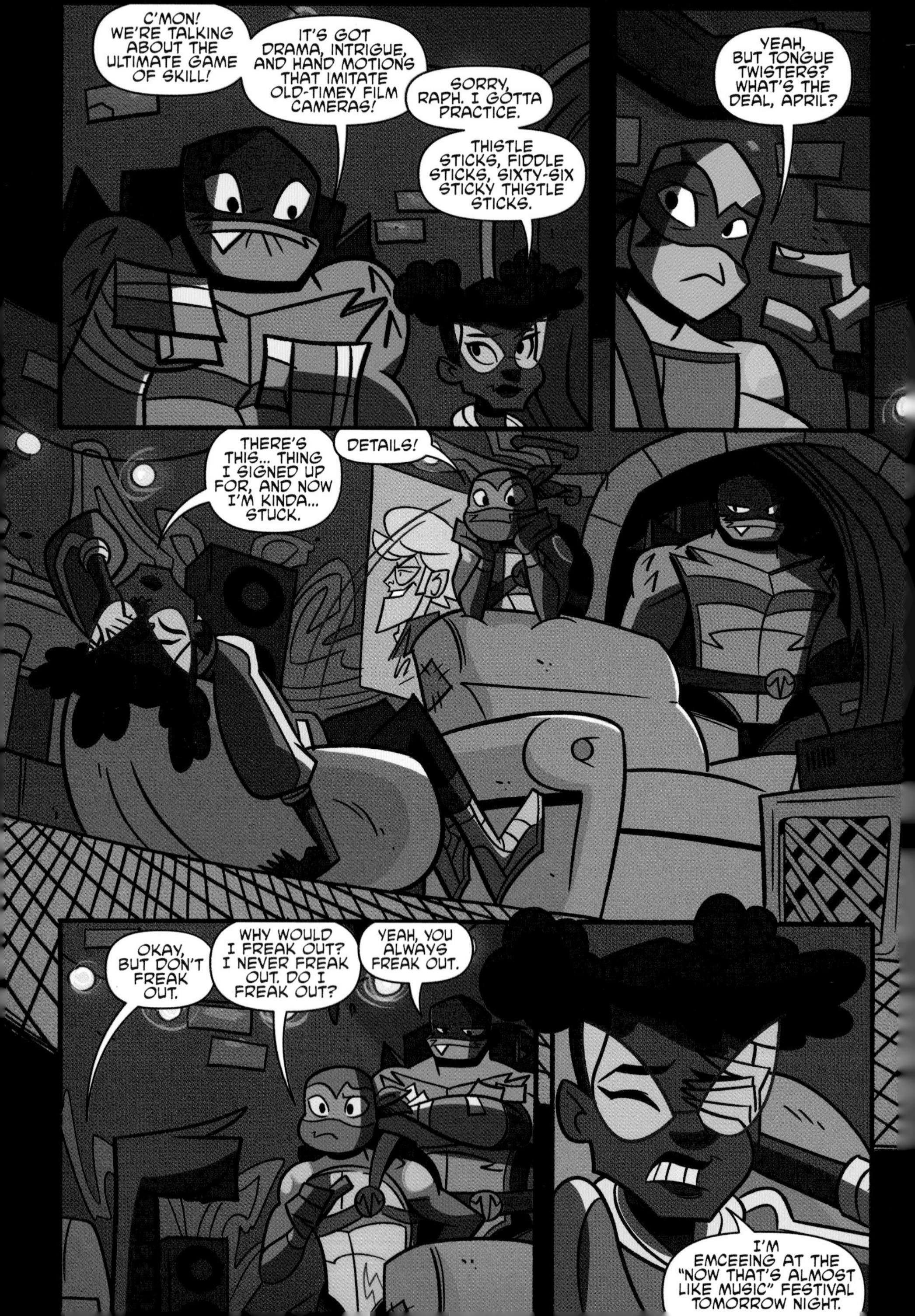
C'MON! WE'RE TALKING ABOUT THE ULTIMATE GAME OF SKILL!
IT'S GOT DRAMA, INTRIGUE, AND HAND MOTIONS THAT IMITATE OLD-TIMEY FILM CAMERAS!
SORRY, RAPH. I GOTTA PRACTICE.
THISTLE STICKS, FIDDLE STICKS, SIXTY-SIX STICKY THISTLE STICKS.
YEAH, BUT TONGUE TWISTERS? WHAT'S THE DEAL, APRIL?
THERE'S THIS... THING I SIGNED UP FOR, AND NOW I'M KINDA... STUCK.
DETAILS!
OKAY, BUT DON'T FREAK OUT.
WHY WOULD I FREAK OUT? I NEVER FREAK OUT. DO I FREAK OUT?
YEAH, YOU ALWAYS FREAK OUT.
I'M EMCEEING AT THE "NOW THAT'S ALMOST LIKE MUSIC" FESTIVAL TOMORROW NIGHT.

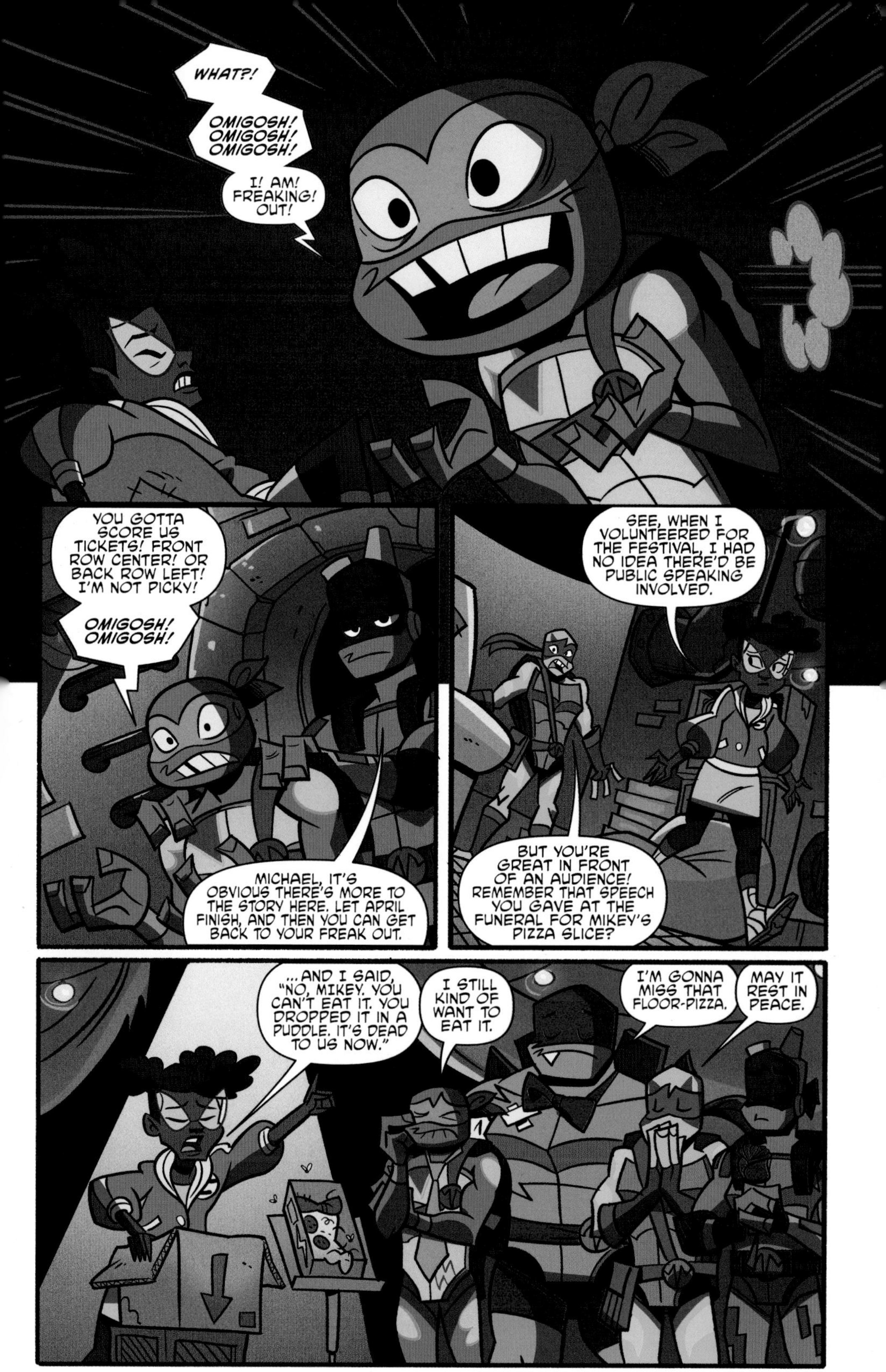
WHAT?!
OMIGOSH! OMIGOSH! OMIGOSH!
I! AM! FREAKING! OUT!
YOU GOTTA SCORE US TICKETS! FRONT ROW CENTER! OR BACK ROW LEFT! I'M NOT PICKY!
OMIGOSH! OMIGOSH!
MICHAEL, IT'S OBVIOUS THERE'S MORE TO THE STORY HERE. LET APRIL FINISH, AND THEN YOU CAN GET BACK TO YOUR FREAK OUT.
SEE, WHEN I VOLUNTEERED FOR THE FESTIVAL, I HAD NO IDEA THERE'D BE PUBLIC SPEAKING INVOLVED.
BUT YOU'RE GREAT IN FRONT OF AN AUDIENCE! REMEMBER THAT SPEECH YOU GAVE AT THE FUNERAL FOR MIKEY'S PIZZA SLICE?
...AND I SAID, "NO, MIKEY. YOU CAN'T EAT IT. YOU DROPPED IT IN A PUDDLE. IT'S DEAD TO US NOW."
I STILL KIND OF WANT TO EAT IT.
I'M GONNA MISS THAT FLOOR-PIZZA.
MAY IT REST IN PEACE.

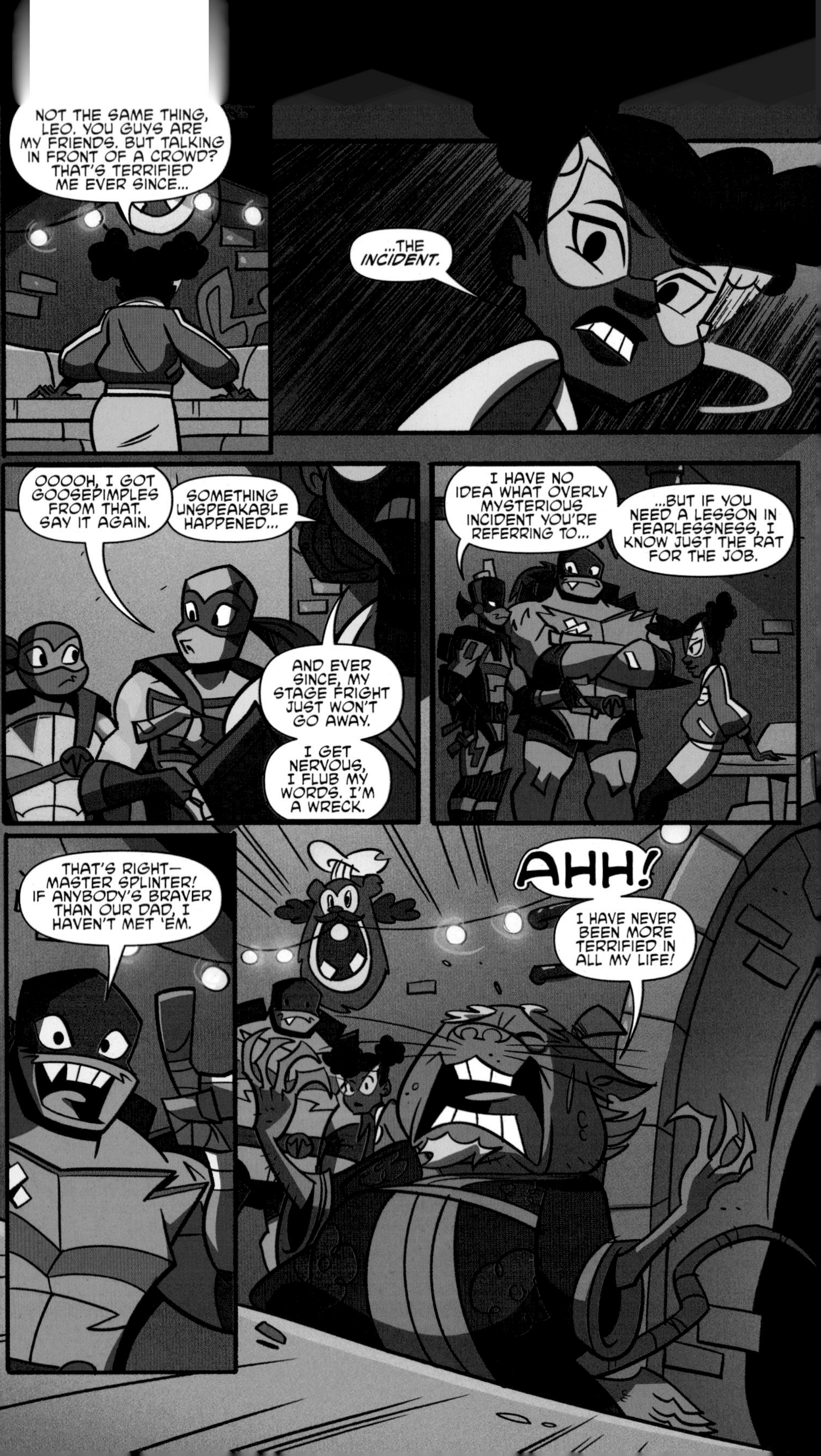
NOT THE SAME THING, LEO. YOU GUYS ARE MY FRIENDS. BUT TALKING IN FRONT OF A CROWD? THAT'S TERRIFIED ME EVER SINCE...
...THE *INCIDENT.*
OOOOH, I GOT GOOSEPIMPLES FROM THAT. SAY IT AGAIN.
SOMETHING UNSPEAKABLE HAPPENED...
AND EVER SINCE, MY STAGE FRIGHT JUST WON'T GO AWAY.
I GET NERVOUS, I FLUB MY WORDS. I'M A WRECK.
I HAVE NO IDEA WHAT OVERLY MYSTERIOUS INCIDENT YOU'RE REFERRING TO...
...BUT IF YOU NEED A LESSON IN FEARLESSNESS, I KNOW JUST THE RAT FOR THE JOB.
THAT'S RIGHT— MASTER SPLINTER! IF ANYBODY'S BRAVER THAN OUR DAD, I HAVEN'T MET 'EM.
AHH!
I HAVE NEVER BEEN MORE TERRIFIED IN ALL MY LIFE!

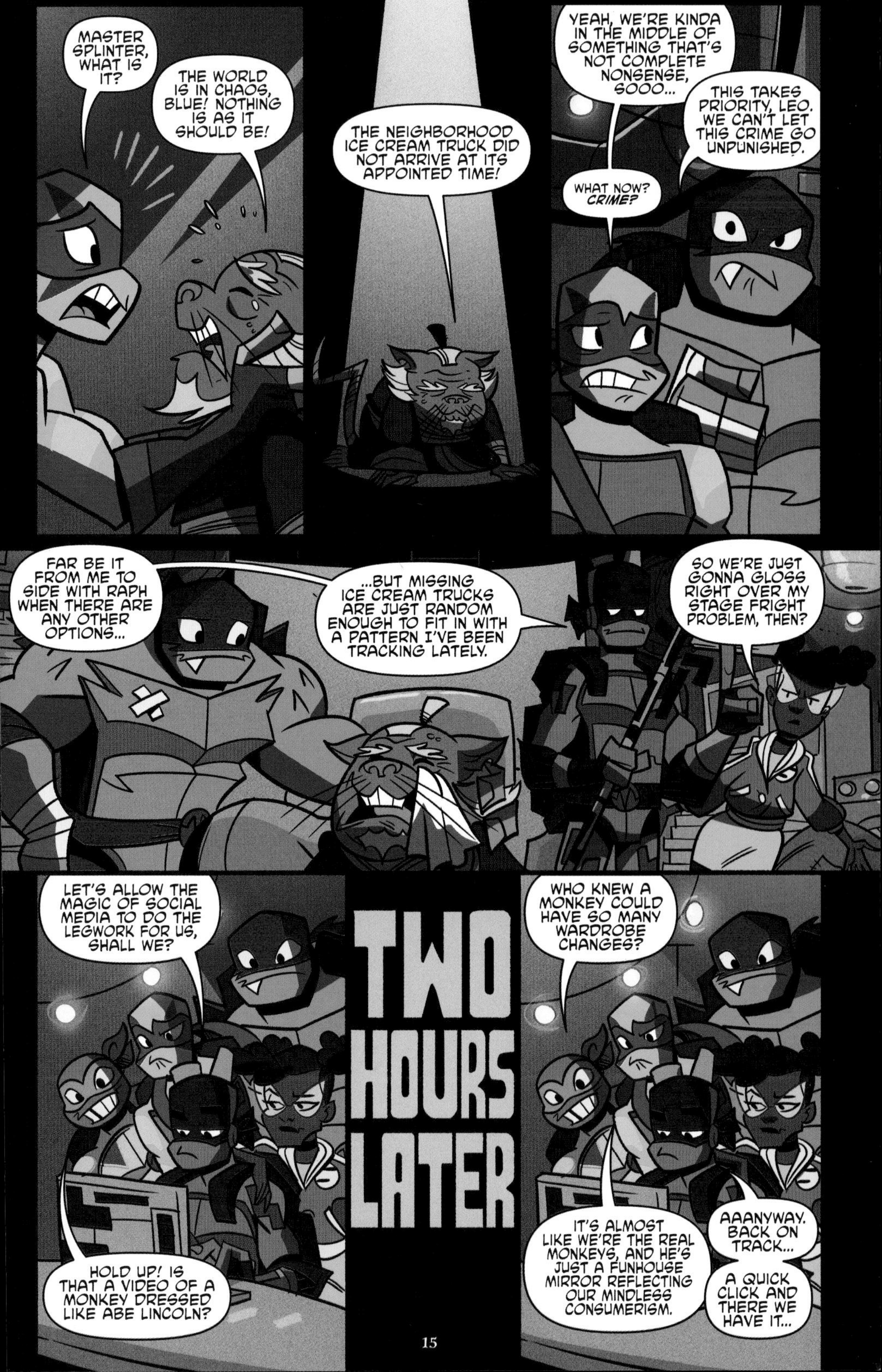
MASTER SPLINTER, WHAT IS IT?
THE WORLD IS IN CHAOS, BLUE! NOTHING IS AS IT SHOULD BE!
THE NEIGHBORHOOD ICE CREAM TRUCK DID NOT ARRIVE AT ITS APPOINTED TIME!
YEAH, WE'RE KINDA IN THE MIDDLE OF SOMETHING THAT'S NOT COMPLETE NONSENSE, SOOO...
THIS TAKES PRIORITY, LEO. WE CAN'T LET THIS CRIME GO UNPUNISHED.
WHAT NOW? *CRIME?*
FAR BE IT FROM ME TO SIDE WITH RAPH WHEN THERE ARE ANY OTHER OPTIONS...
...BUT MISSING ICE CREAM TRUCKS ARE JUST RANDOM ENOUGH TO FIT IN WITH A PATTERN I'VE BEEN TRACKING LATELY.
SO WE'RE JUST GONNA GLOSS RIGHT OVER MY STAGE FRIGHT PROBLEM, THEN?
LET'S ALLOW THE MAGIC OF SOCIAL MEDIA TO DO THE LEGWORK FOR US, SHALL WE?
HOLD UP! IS THAT A VIDEO OF A MONKEY DRESSED LIKE ABE LINCOLN?
TWO HOURS LATER
WHO KNEW A MONKEY COULD HAVE SO MANY WARDROBE CHANGES?
IT'S ALMOST LIKE WE'RE THE REAL MONKEYS, AND HE'S JUST A FUNHOUSE MIRROR REFLECTING OUR MINDLESS CONSUMERISM.
AAANYWAY. BACK ON TRACK...
A QUICK CLICK AND THERE WE HAVE IT...

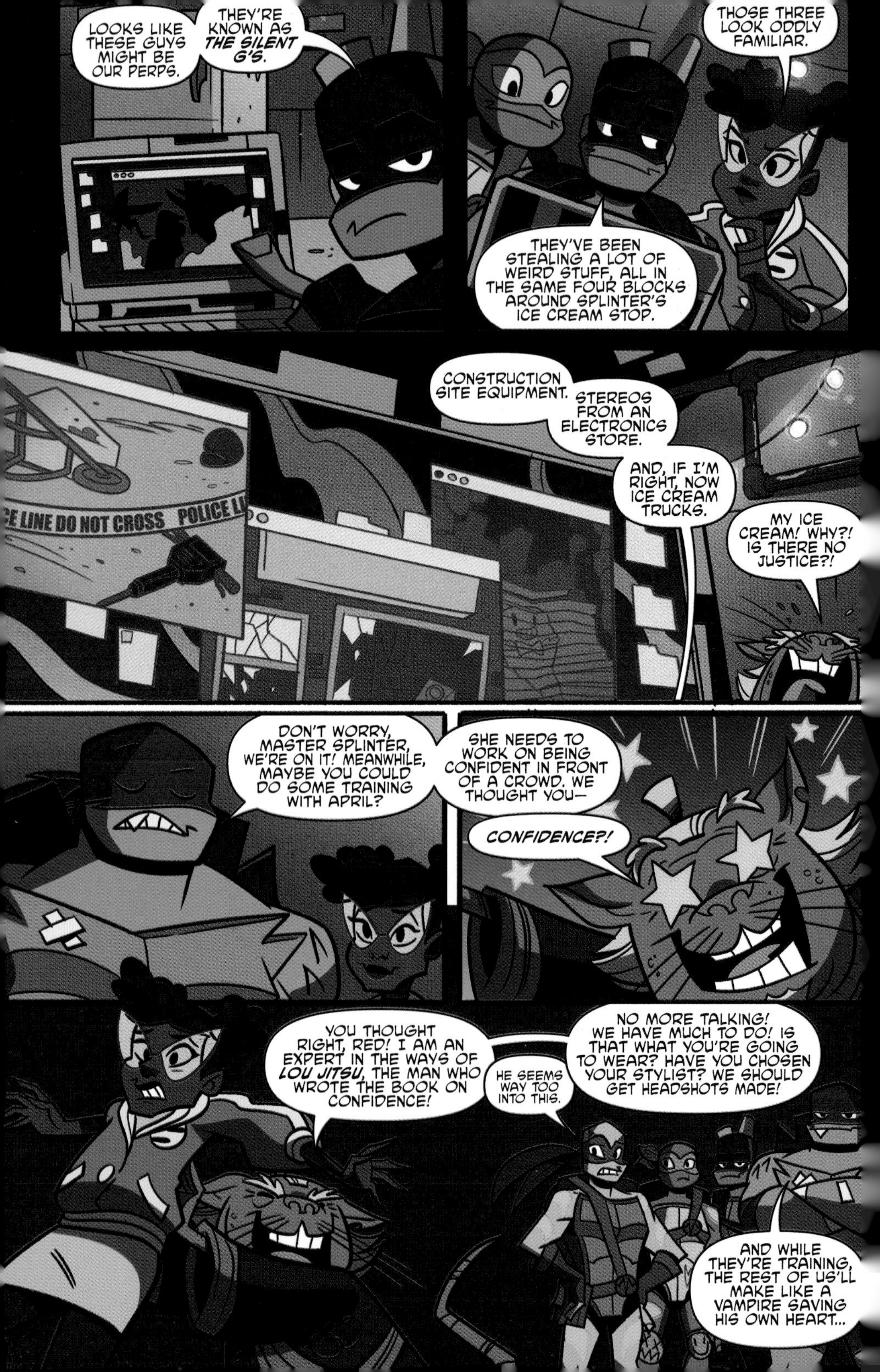
LOOKS LIKE THESE GUYS MIGHT BE OUR PERPS.
THEY'RE KNOWN AS THE SILENT G'S.
THOSE THREE LOOK ODDLY FAMILIAR.
THEY'VE BEEN STEALING A LOT OF WEIRD STUFF, ALL IN THE SAME FOUR BLOCKS AROUND SPLINTER'S ICE CREAM STOP.
POLICE LINE DO NOT CROSS POLICE LI
CONSTRUCTION SITE EQUIPMENT.
STEREOS FROM AN ELECTRONICS STORE.
AND, IF I'M RIGHT, NOW ICE CREAM TRUCKS.
MY ICE CREAM! WHY?! IS THERE NO JUSTICE?!
DON'T WORRY, MASTER SPLINTER, WE'RE ON IT! MEANWHILE, MAYBE YOU COULD DO SOME TRAINING WITH APRIL?
SHE NEEDS TO WORK ON BEING CONFIDENT IN FRONT OF A CROWD. WE THOUGHT YOU—
CONFIDENCE?!
YOU THOUGHT RIGHT, RED! I AM AN EXPERT IN THE WAYS OF LOU JITSU, THE MAN WHO WROTE THE BOOK ON CONFIDENCE!
HE SEEMS WAY TOO INTO THIS.
NO MORE TALKING! WE HAVE MUCH TO DO! IS THAT WHAT YOU'RE GOING TO WEAR? HAVE YOU CHOSEN YOUR STYLIST? WE SHOULD GET HEADSHOTS MADE!
AND WHILE THEY'RE TRAINING, THE REST OF US'LL MAKE LIKE A VAMPIRE SAVING HIS OWN HEART...

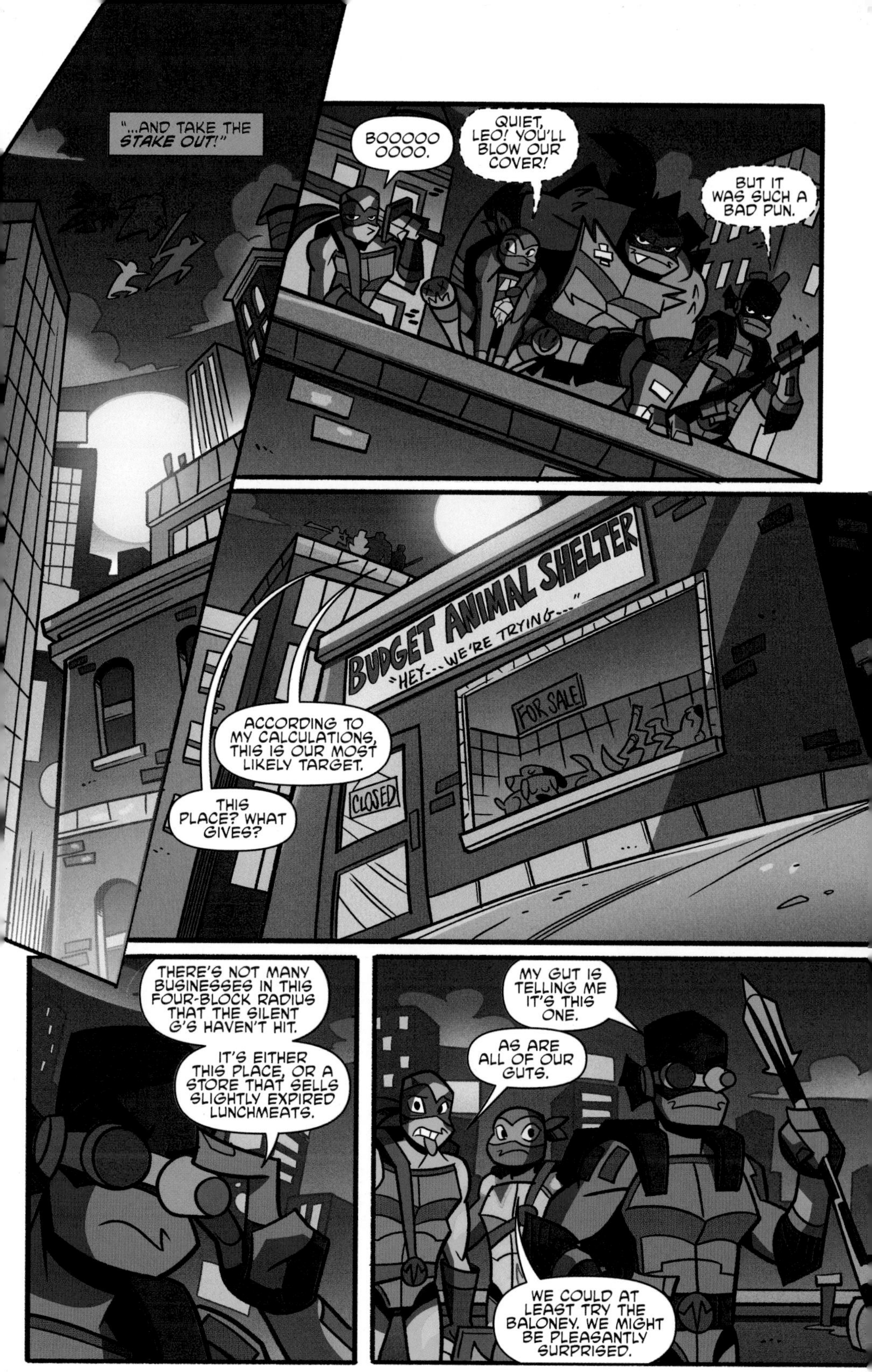
"...AND TAKE THE STAKE OUT!"
BOOOOO OOOO.
QUIET, LEO! YOU'LL BLOW OUR COVER!
BUT IT WAS SUCH A BAD PUN.
BUDGET ANIMAL SHELTER
"HEY... WE'RE TRYING..."
FOR SALE
CLOSED
ACCORDING TO MY CALCULATIONS, THIS IS OUR MOST LIKELY TARGET.
THIS PLACE? WHAT GIVES?
THERE'S NOT MANY BUSINESSES IN THIS FOUR-BLOCK RADIUS THAT THE SILENT G'S HAVEN'T HIT.
IT'S EITHER THIS PLACE, OR A STORE THAT SELLS SLIGHTLY EXPIRED LUNCHMEATS.
MY GUT IS TELLING ME IT'S THIS ONE.
AS ARE ALL OF OUR GUTS.
WE COULD AT LEAST TRY THE BALONEY. WE MIGHT BE PLEASANTLY SURPRISED.

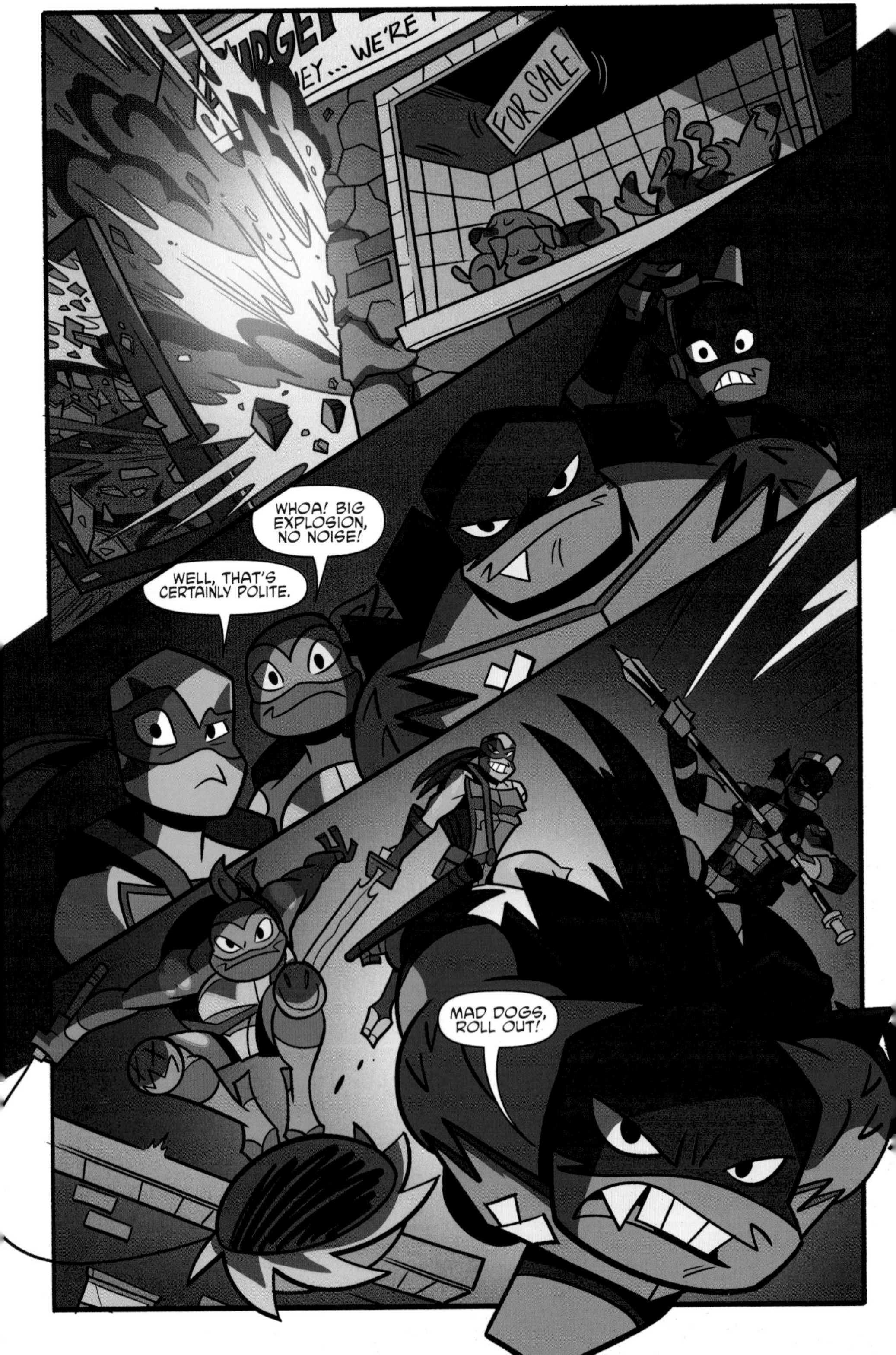

FOR SALE
WHOA! BIG EXPLOSION, NO NOISE!
WELL, THAT'S CERTAINLY POLITE.
MAD DOGS, ROLL OUT!

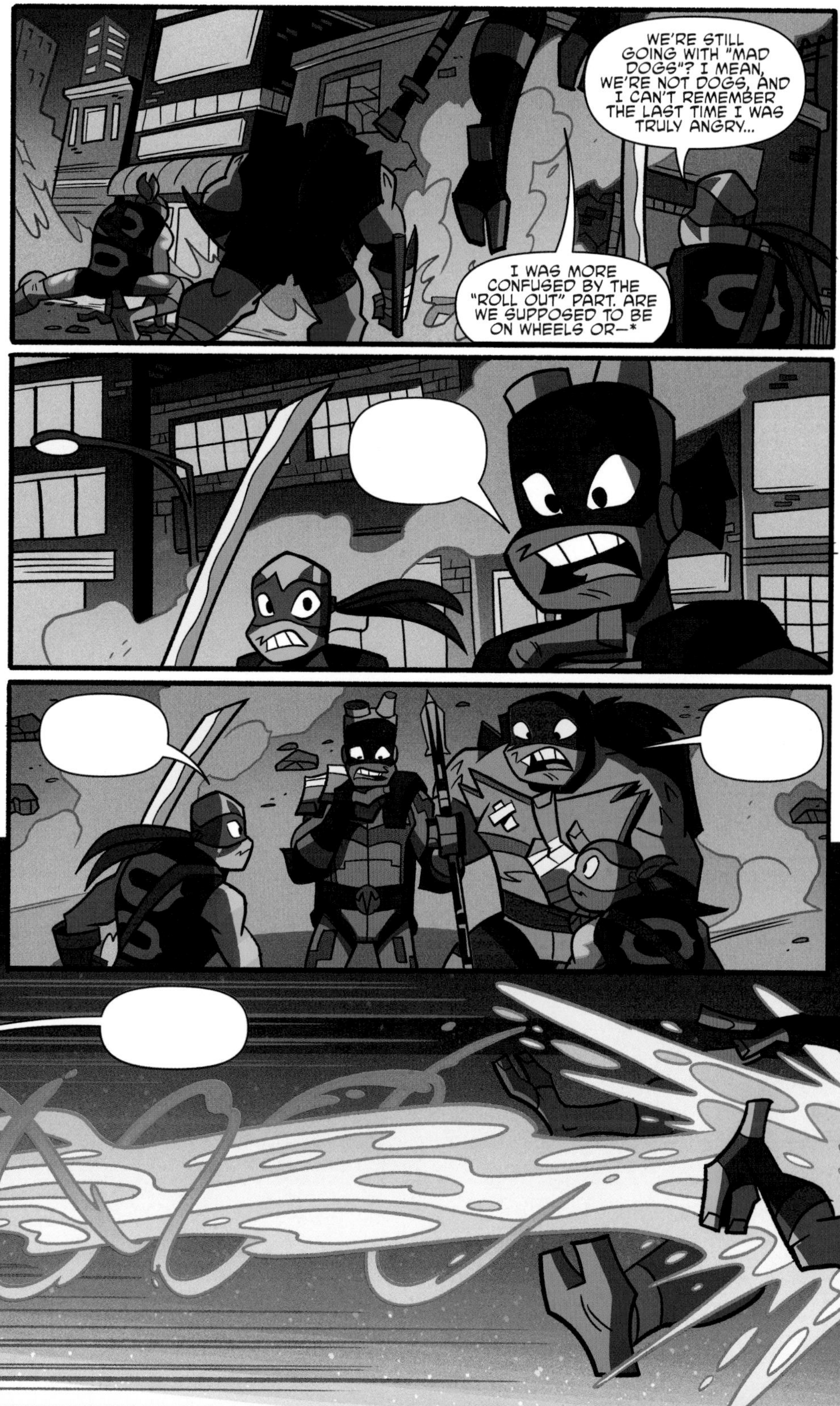
WE'RE STILL GOING WITH "MAD DOGS"? I MEAN, WE'RE NOT DOGS, AND I CAN'T REMEMBER THE LAST TIME I WAS TRULY ANGRY...
I WAS MORE CONFUSED BY THE "ROLL OUT" PART. ARE WE SUPPOSED TO BE ON WHEELS OR—*

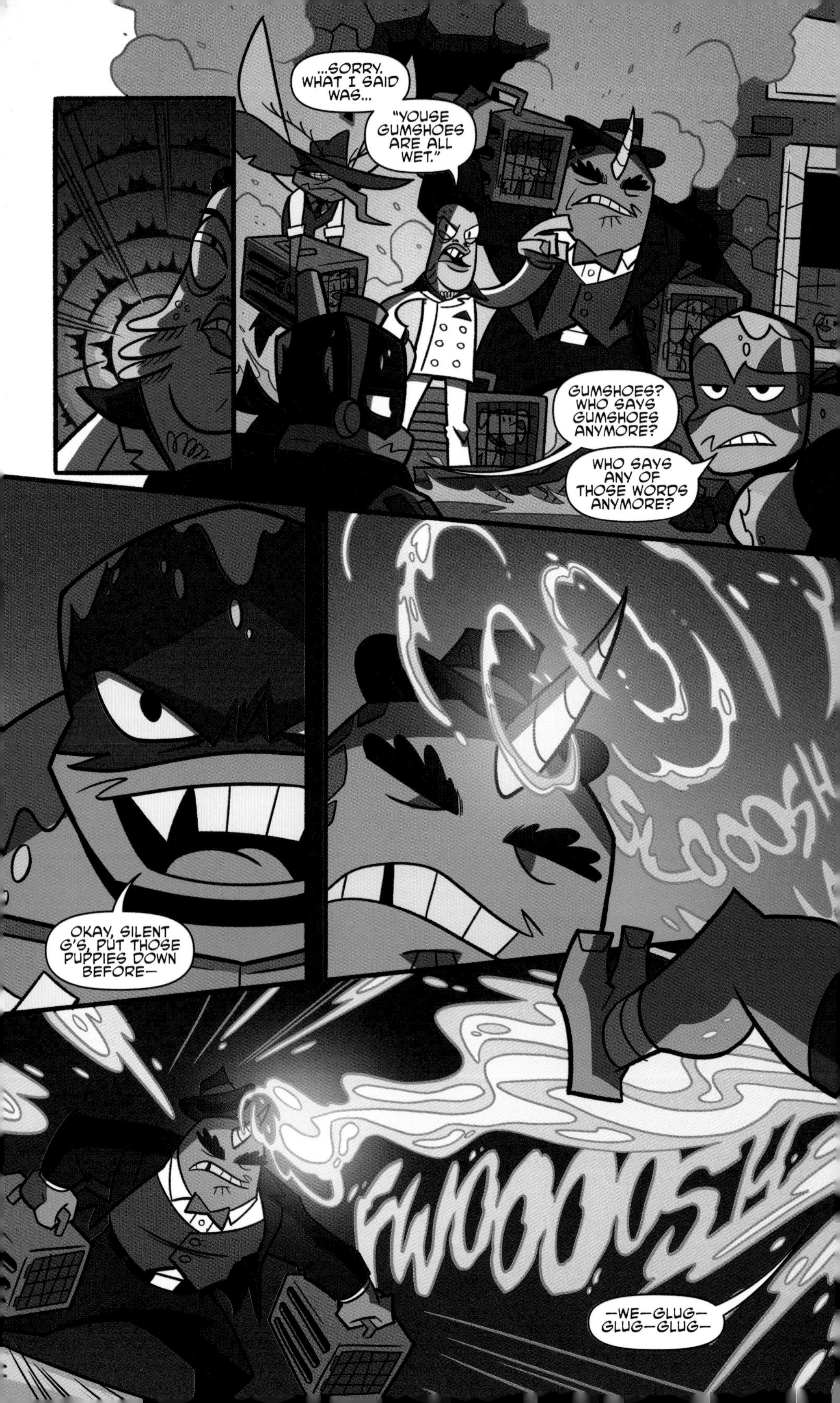
...SORRY. WHAT I SAID WAS...
"YOUSE GUMSHOES ARE ALL WET."
GUMSHOES? WHO SAYS GUMSHOES ANYMORE?
WHO SAYS ANY OF THOSE WORDS ANYMORE?
OKAY, SILENT G'S, PUT THOSE PUPPIES DOWN BEFORE—
SLOOOSH
FWOOOSH
—WE—GLUG—GLUG—GLUG—

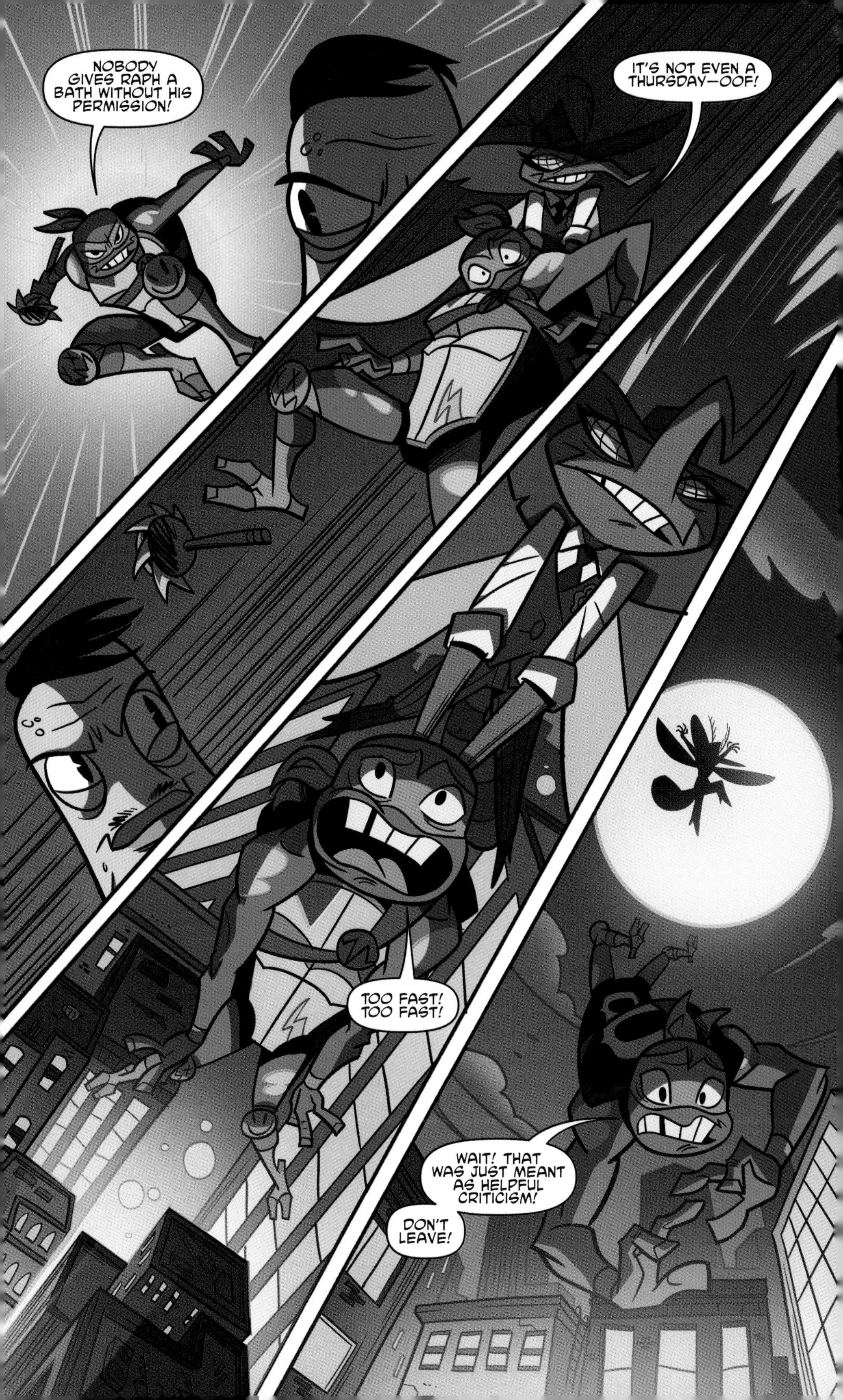
NOBODY GIVES RAPH A BATH WITHOUT HIS PERMISSION!
IT'S NOT EVEN A THURSDAY—OOF!
TOO FAST! TOO FAST!
WAIT! THAT WAS JUST MEANT AS HELPFUL CRITICISM!
DON'T LEAVE!

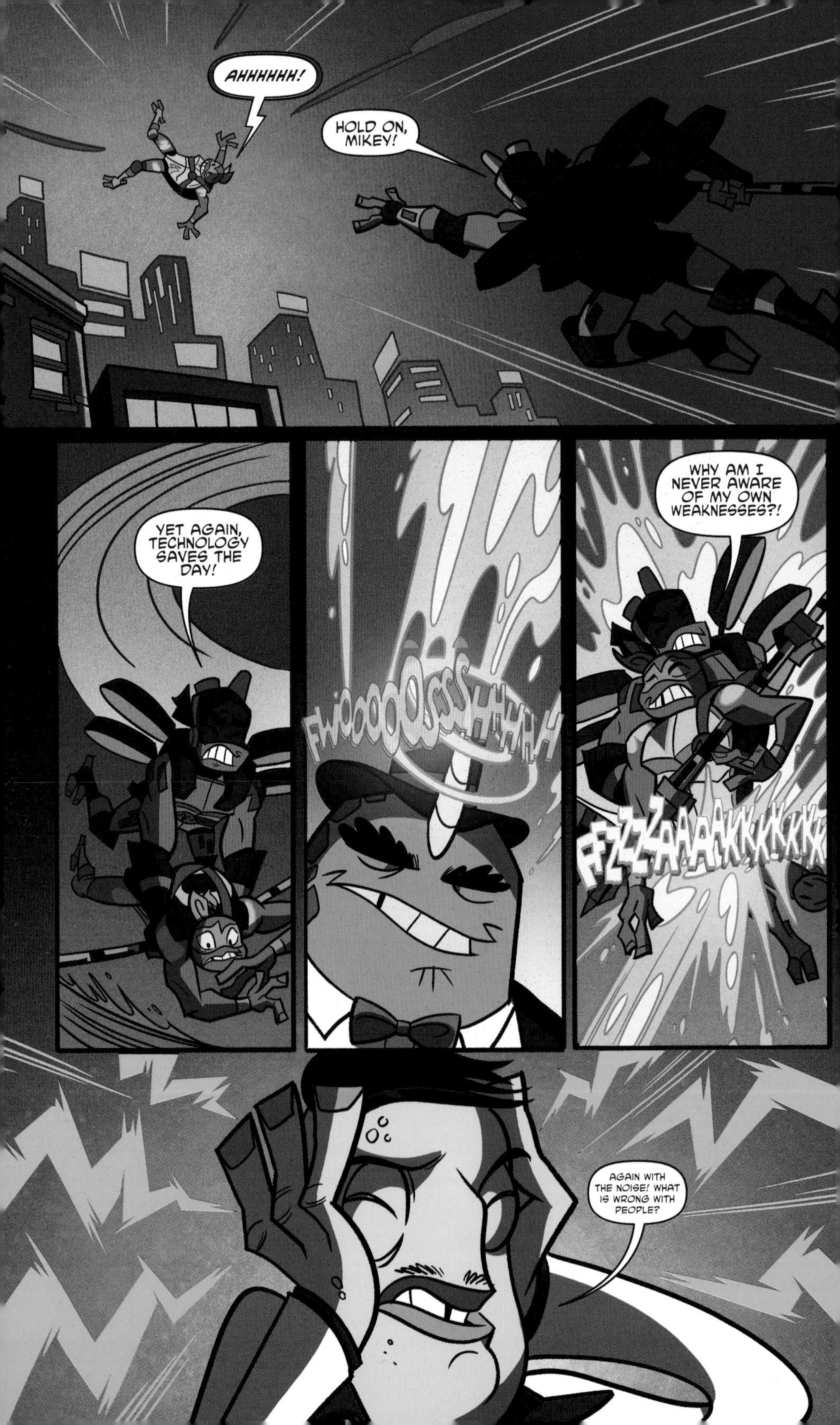
AHHHHHH!
HOLD ON, MIKEY!
YET AGAIN, TECHNOLOGY SAVES THE DAY!
FWOOOOOSSSHHHH
WHY AM I NEVER AWARE OF MY OWN WEAKNESSES?!
FZZZAAAAKKKKKK
AGAIN WITH THE NOISE! WHAT IS WRONG WITH PEOPLE?

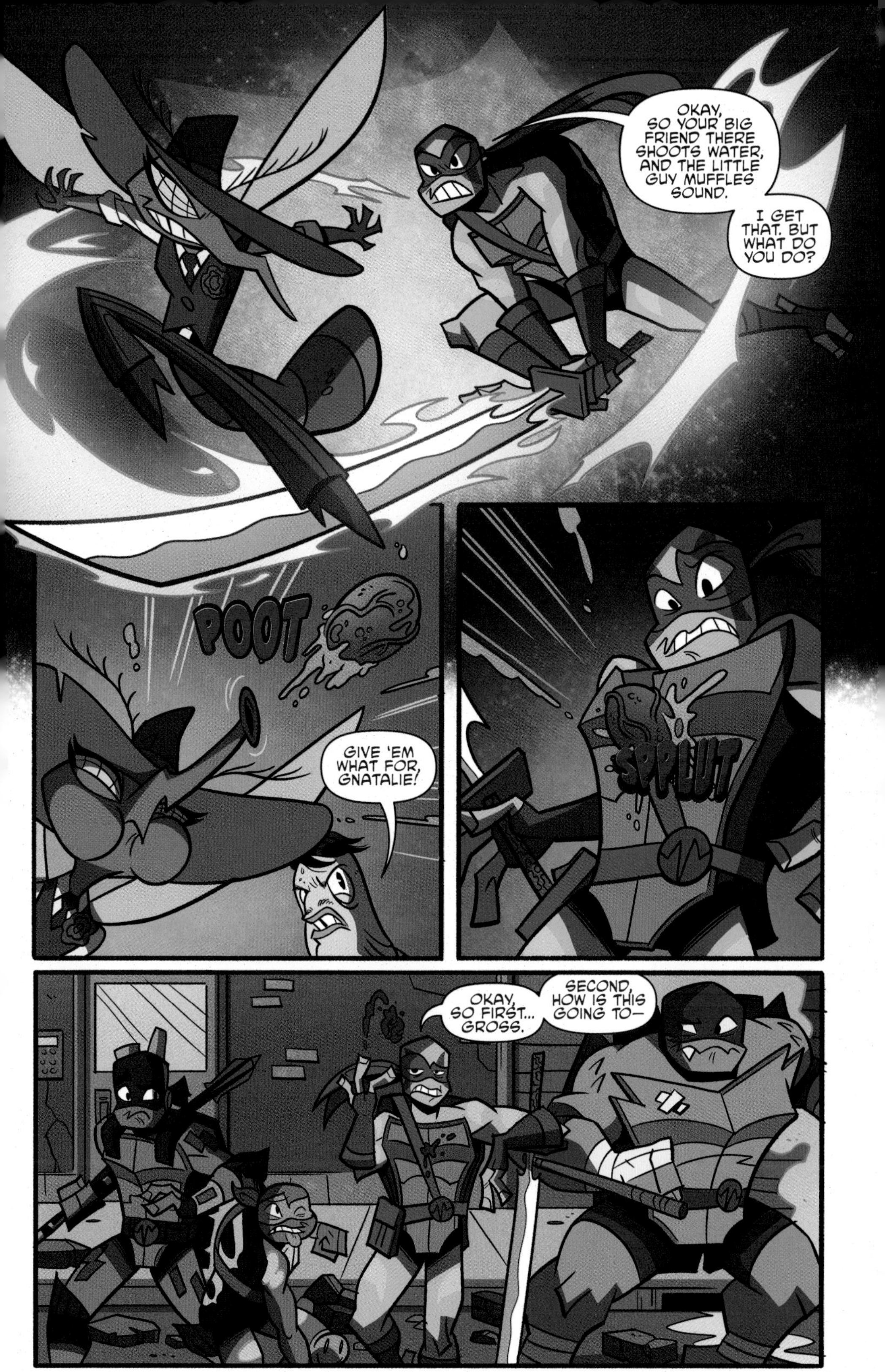
OKAY, SO YOUR BIG FRIEND THERE SHOOTS WATER, AND THE LITTLE GUY MUFFLES SOUND.
I GET THAT. BUT WHAT DO YOU DO?
POOT
GIVE 'EM WHAT FOR, GNATALIE!
SPPLUT
OKAY, SO FIRST... GROSS.
SECOND, HOW IS THIS GOING TO—

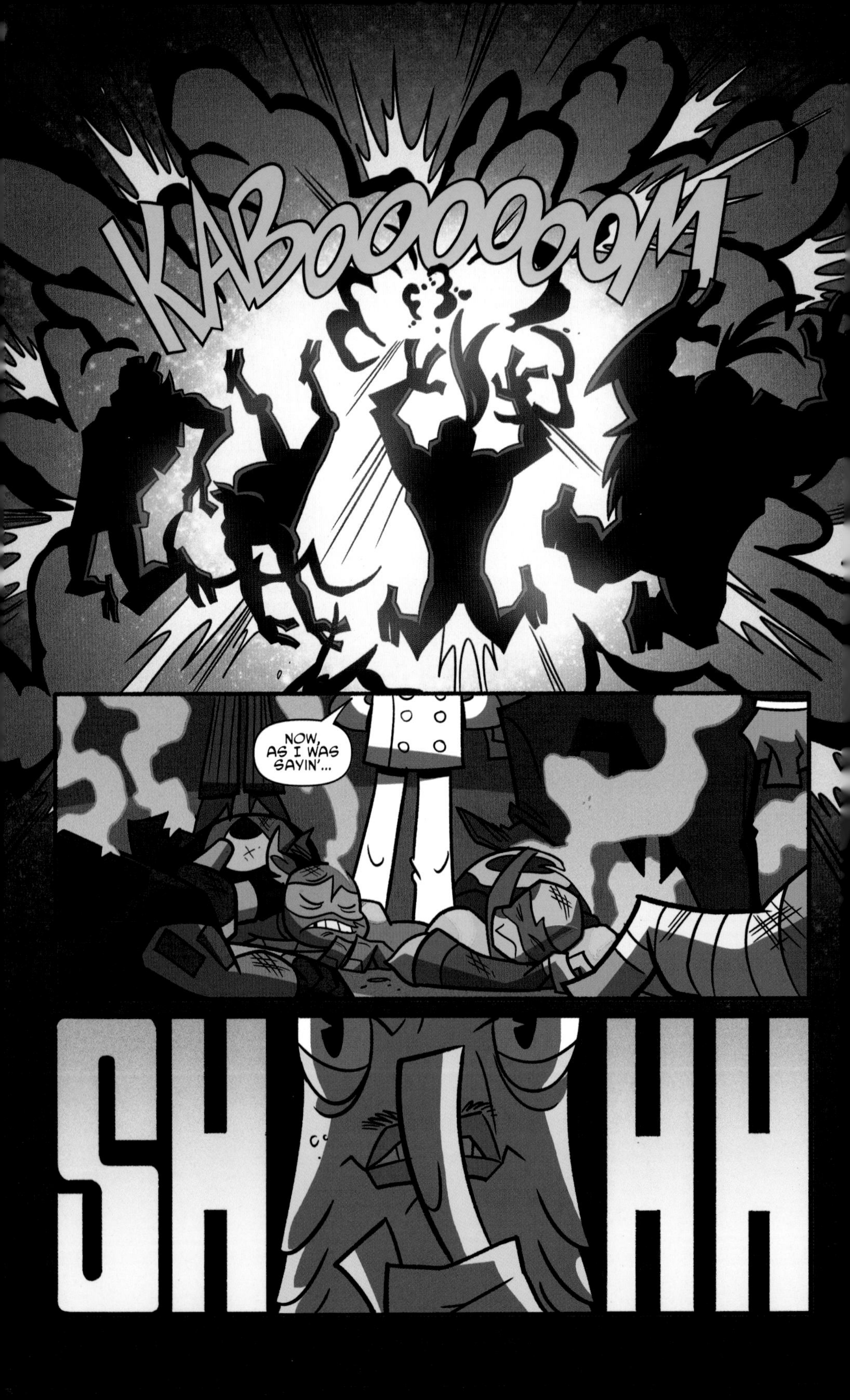
KABOOOOOOM
NOW, AS I WAS SAYIN'...
SH HH

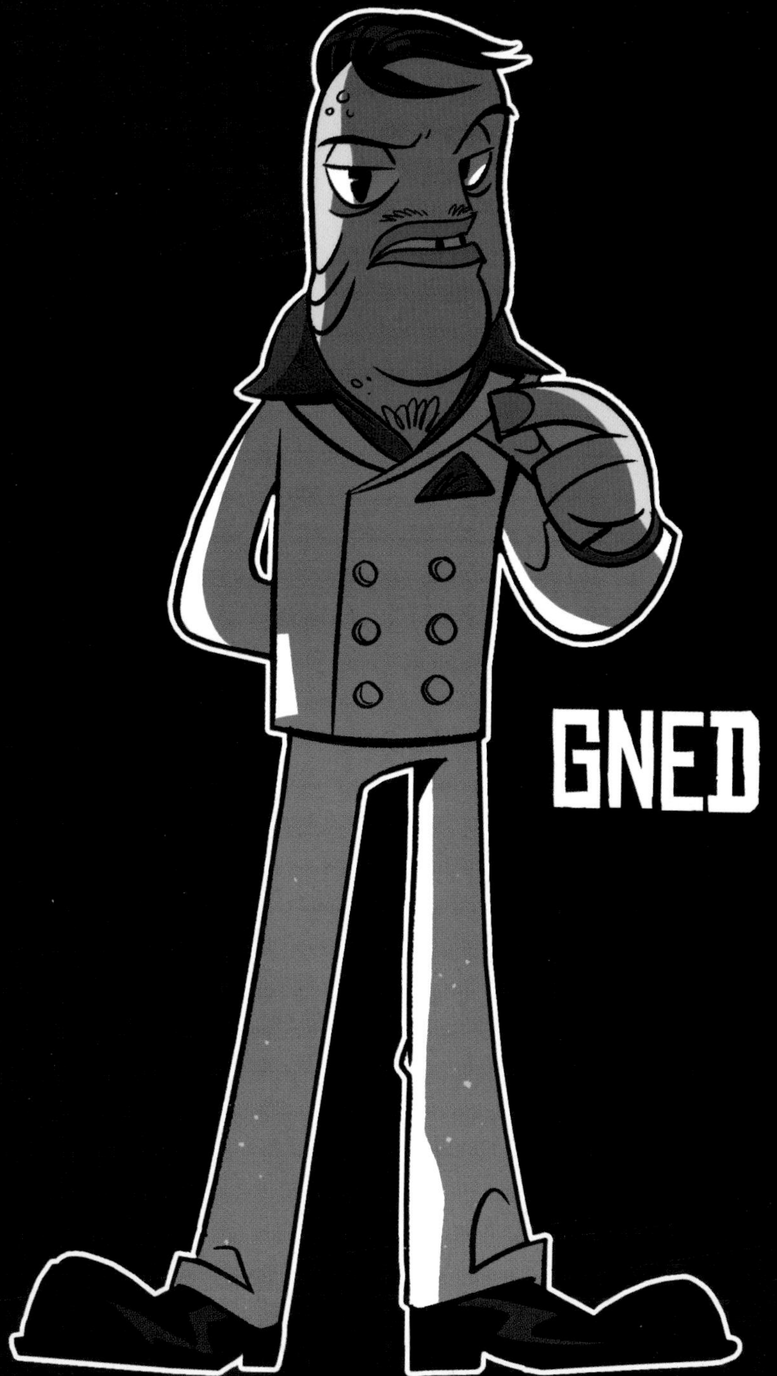
GNED

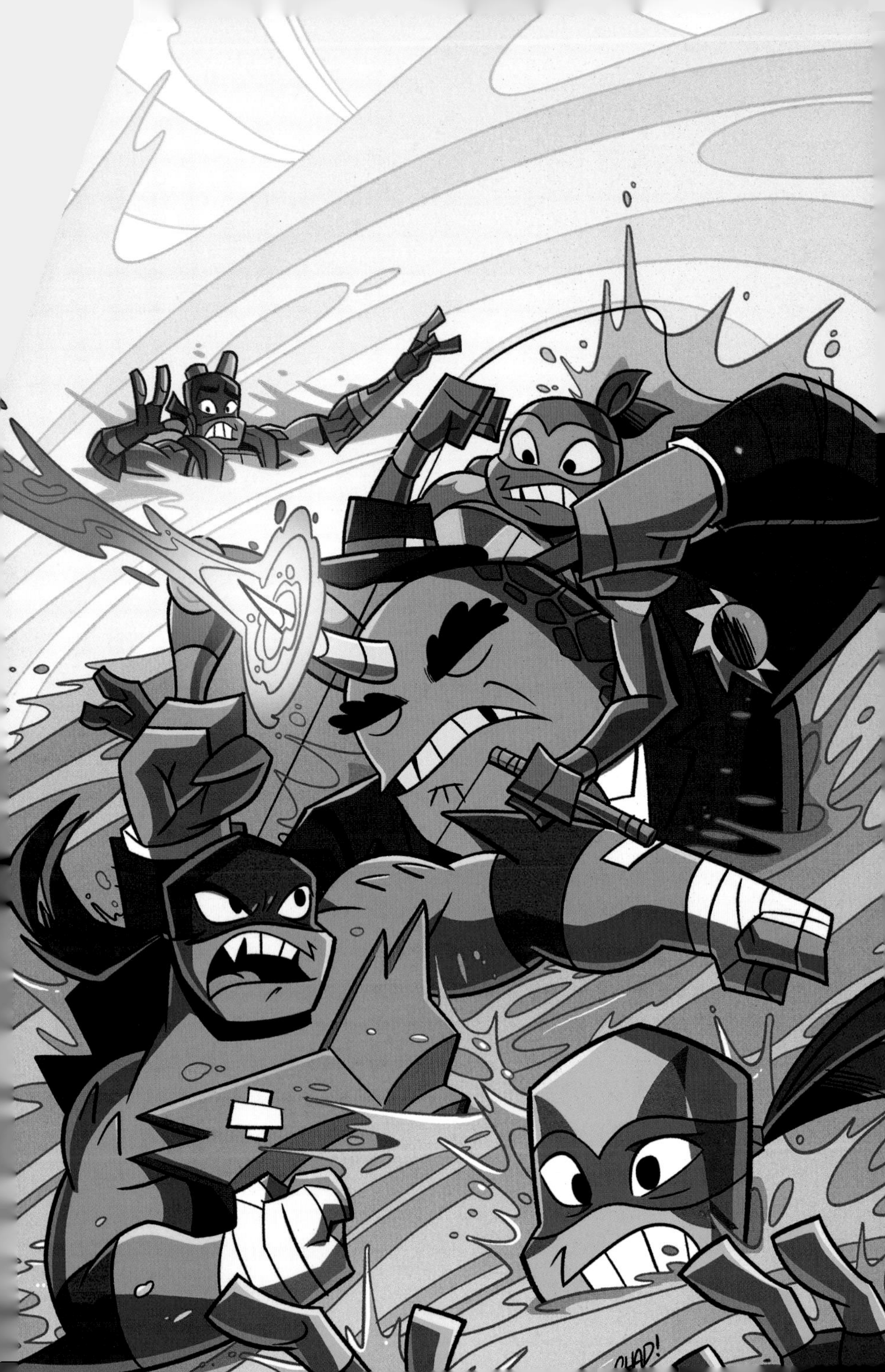
CHAD!

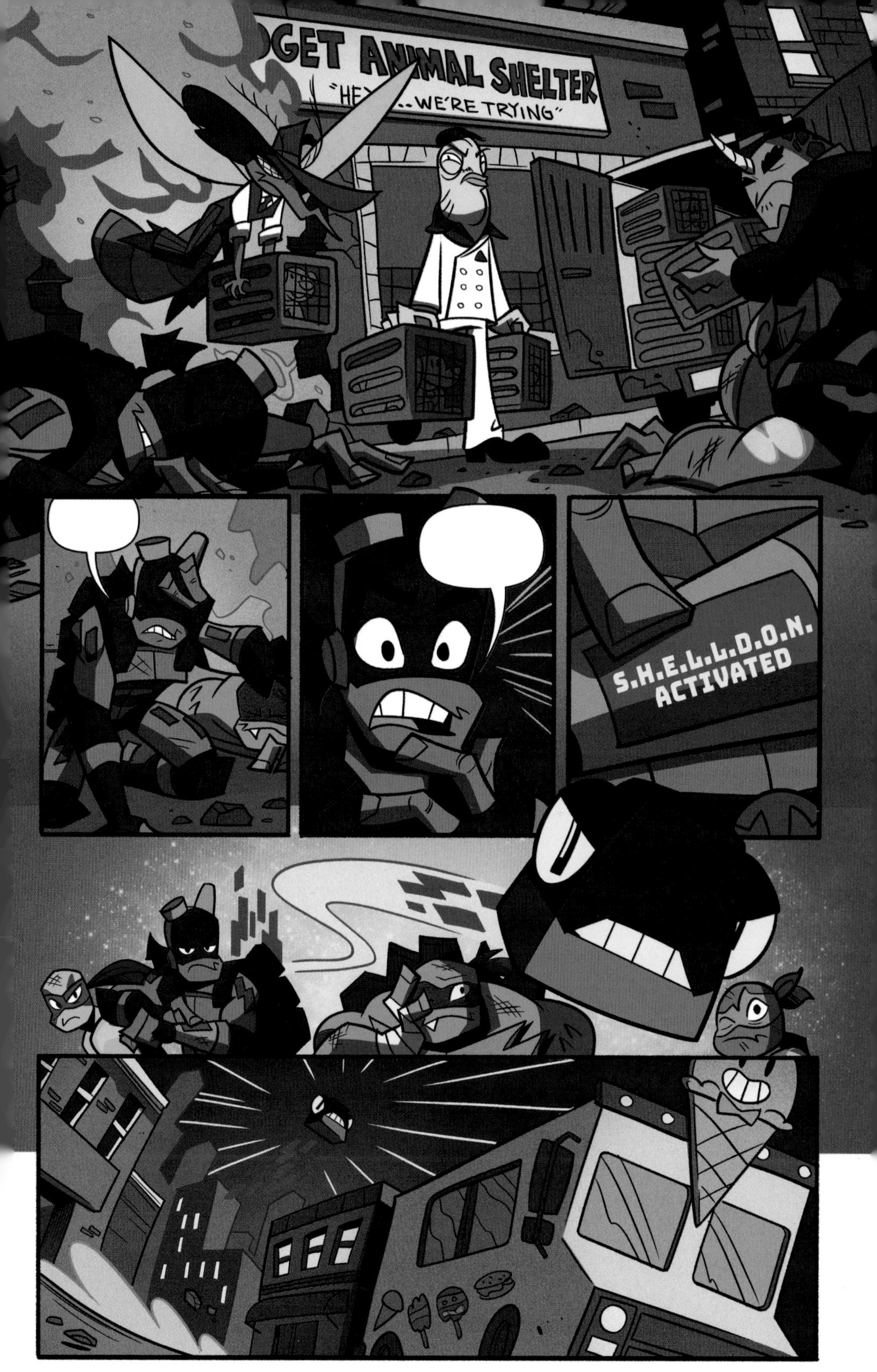
GET ANIMAL SHELTER
"HEY... WE'RE TRYING"
S.H.E.L.L.D.O.N. ACTIVATED

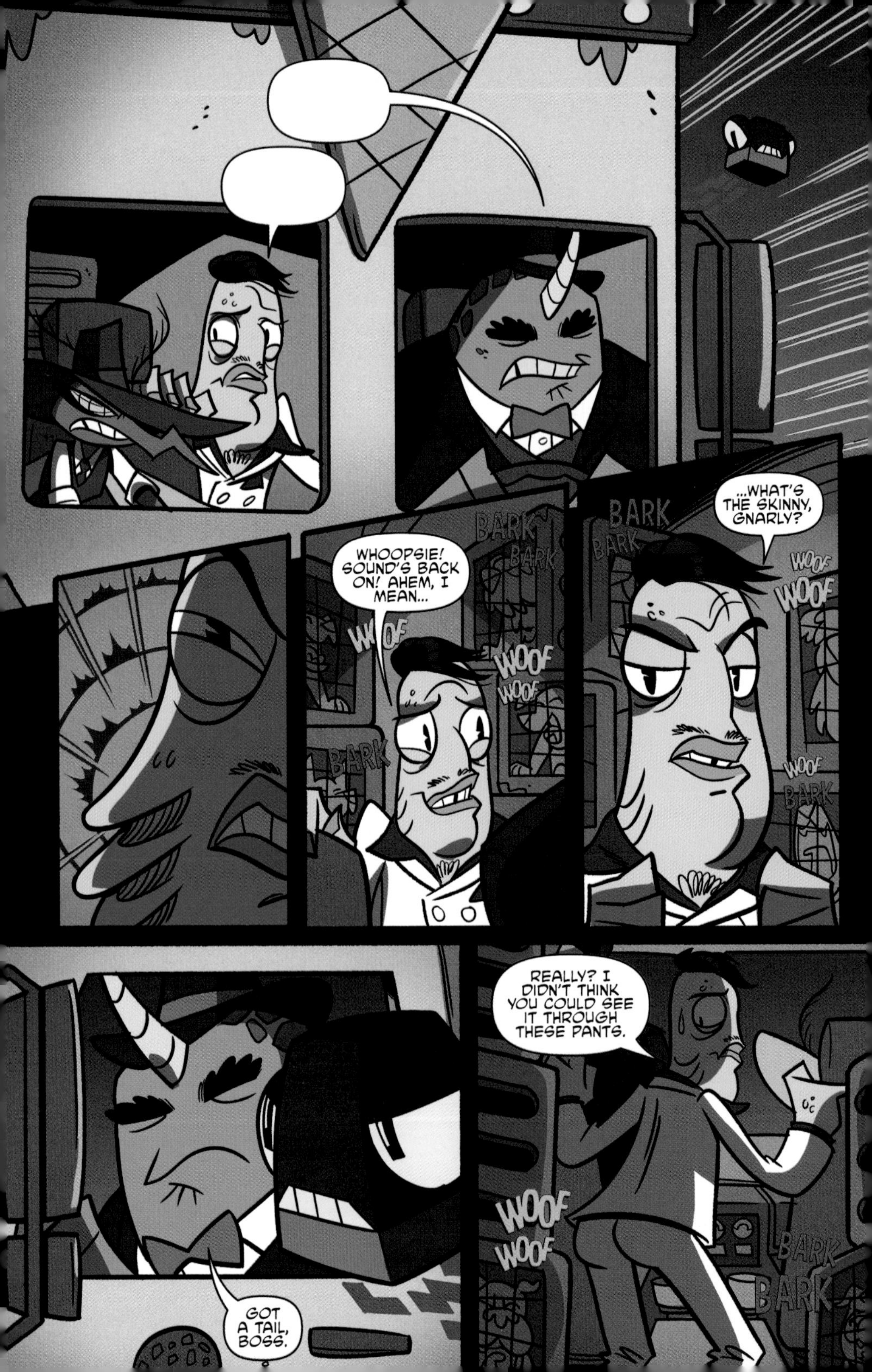
BARK
BARK
WHOOPSIE! SOUND'S BACK ON! AHEM, I MEAN...
WOOF
WOOF
WOOF
BARK
BARK
BARK
...WHAT'S THE SKINNY, GNARLY?
WOOF
WOOF
WOOF
BARK
GOT A TAIL, BOSS.
REALLY? I DIDN'T THINK YOU COULD SEE IT THROUGH THESE PANTS.
WOOF
WOOF
BARK
BARK

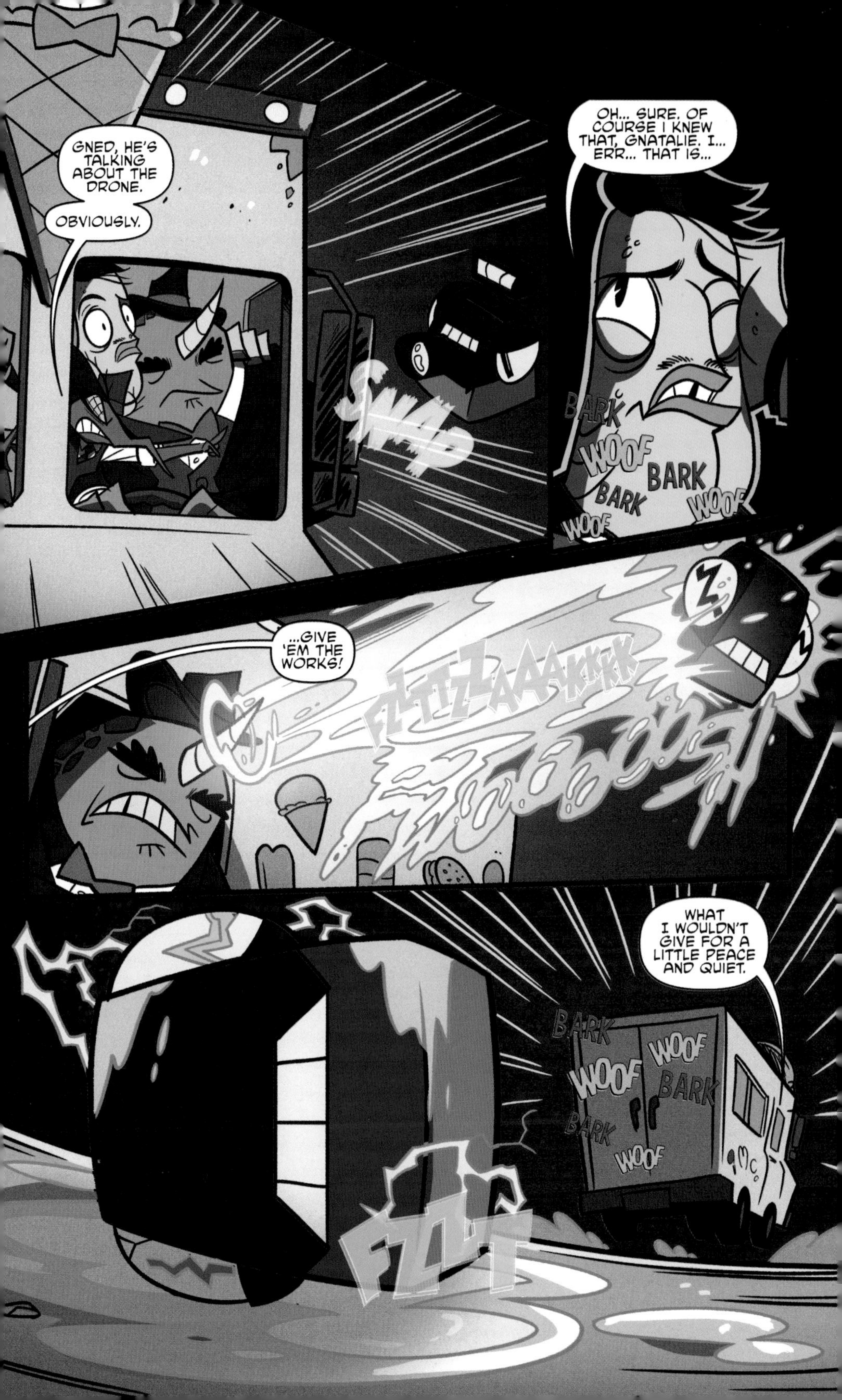
GNED, HE'S TALKING ABOUT THE DRONE.
OBVIOUSLY.
SNAP
OH... SURE. OF COURSE I KNEW THAT, GNATALIE. I... ERR... THAT IS...
BARK
WOOF
BARK
BARK
WOOF
WOOF
...GIVE 'EM THE WORKS!
FZZTTZZAAAKKKK
FWOOOOOOSH
WHAT I WOULDN'T GIVE FOR A LITTLE PEACE AND QUIET.
BARK
WOOF
WOOF
BARK
BARK
WOOF
FZZT

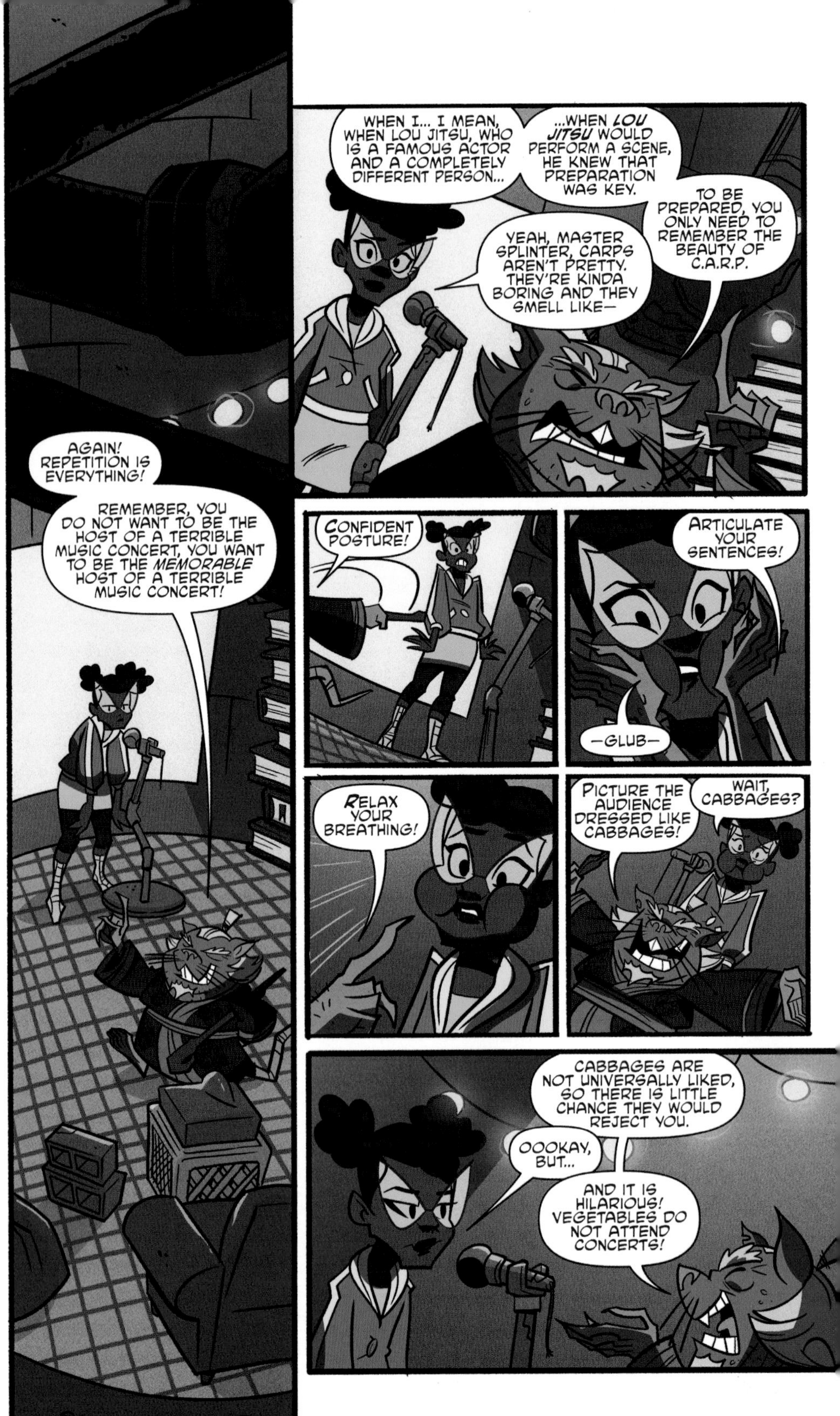
AGAIN! REPETITION IS EVERYTHING!
REMEMBER, YOU DO NOT WANT TO BE THE HOST OF A TERRIBLE MUSIC CONCERT, YOU WANT TO BE THE *MEMORABLE* HOST OF A TERRIBLE MUSIC CONCERT!
WHEN I... I MEAN, WHEN LOU JITSU, WHO IS A FAMOUS ACTOR AND A COMPLETELY DIFFERENT PERSON...
...WHEN *LOU JITSU* WOULD PERFORM A SCENE, HE KNEW THAT PREPARATION WAS KEY.
TO BE PREPARED, YOU ONLY NEED TO REMEMBER THE BEAUTY OF C.A.R.P.
YEAH, MASTER SPLINTER, CARPS AREN'T PRETTY. THEY'RE KINDA BORING AND THEY SMELL LIKE—
CONFIDENT POSTURE!
ARTICULATE YOUR SENTENCES!
—GLUB—
RELAX YOUR BREATHING!
PICTURE THE AUDIENCE DRESSED LIKE CABBAGES!
WAIT, CABBAGES?
CABBAGES ARE NOT UNIVERSALLY LIKED, SO THERE IS LITTLE CHANCE THEY WOULD REJECT YOU.
OOOKAY, BUT...
AND IT IS HILARIOUS! VEGETABLES DO NOT ATTEND CONCERTS!

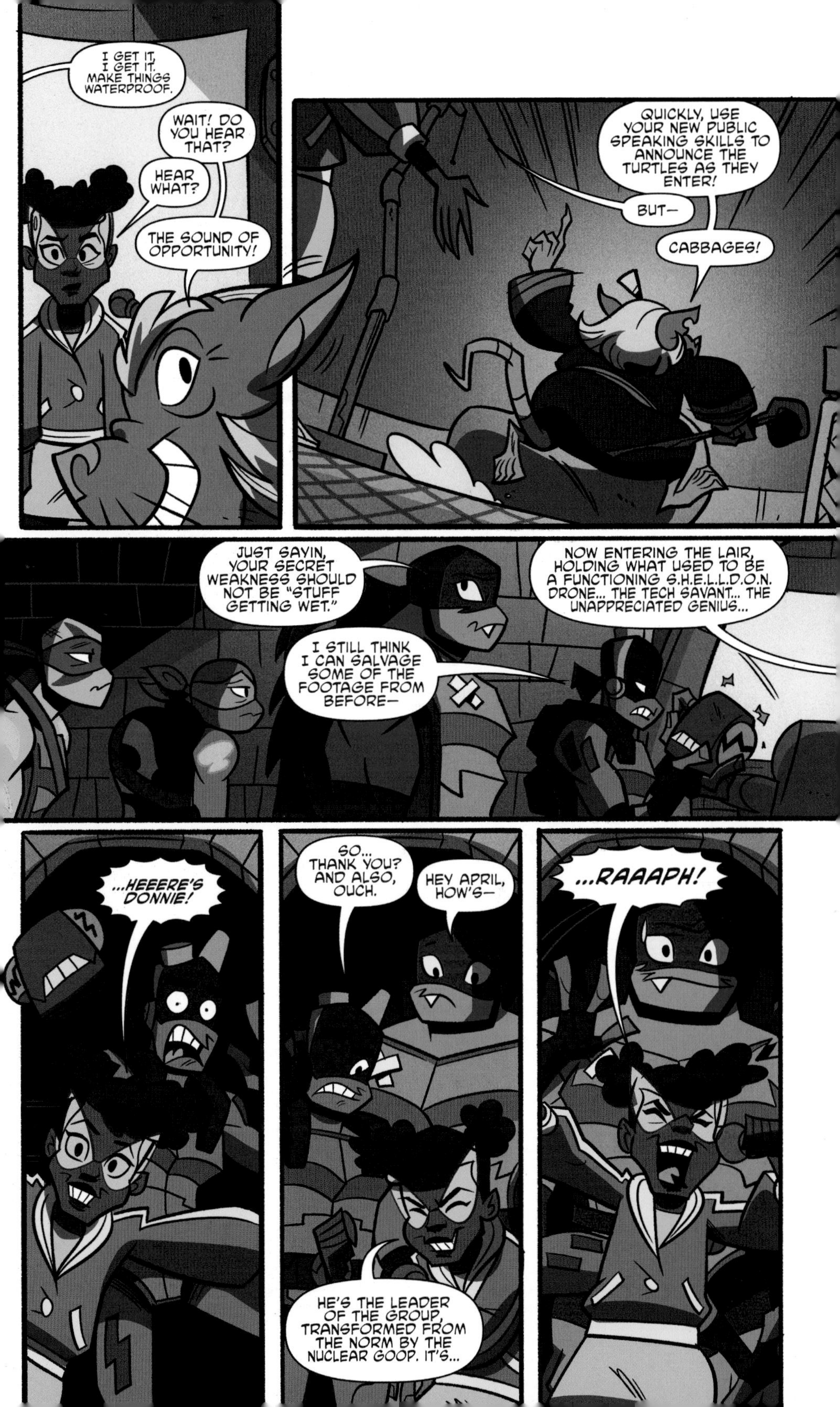

I GET IT, I GET IT. MAKE THINGS WATERPROOF.
WAIT! DO YOU HEAR THAT?
HEAR WHAT?
THE SOUND OF OPPORTUNITY!
QUICKLY, USE YOUR NEW PUBLIC SPEAKING SKILLS TO ANNOUNCE THE TURTLES AS THEY ENTER!
BUT—
CABBAGES!
JUST SAYIN, YOUR SECRET WEAKNESS SHOULD NOT BE "STUFF GETTING WET."
NOW ENTERING THE LAIR, HOLDING WHAT USED TO BE A FUNCTIONING S.H.E.L.L.D.O.N. DRONE... THE TECH SAVANT... THE UNAPPRECIATED GENIUS...
I STILL THINK I CAN SALVAGE SOME OF THE FOOTAGE FROM BEFORE—
...HEEERE'S DONNIE!
SO... THANK YOU? AND ALSO, OUCH.
HEY APRIL, HOW'S—
HE'S THE LEADER OF THE GROUP, TRANSFORMED FROM THE NORM BY THE NUCLEAR GOOP. IT'S...
...RAAAPH!

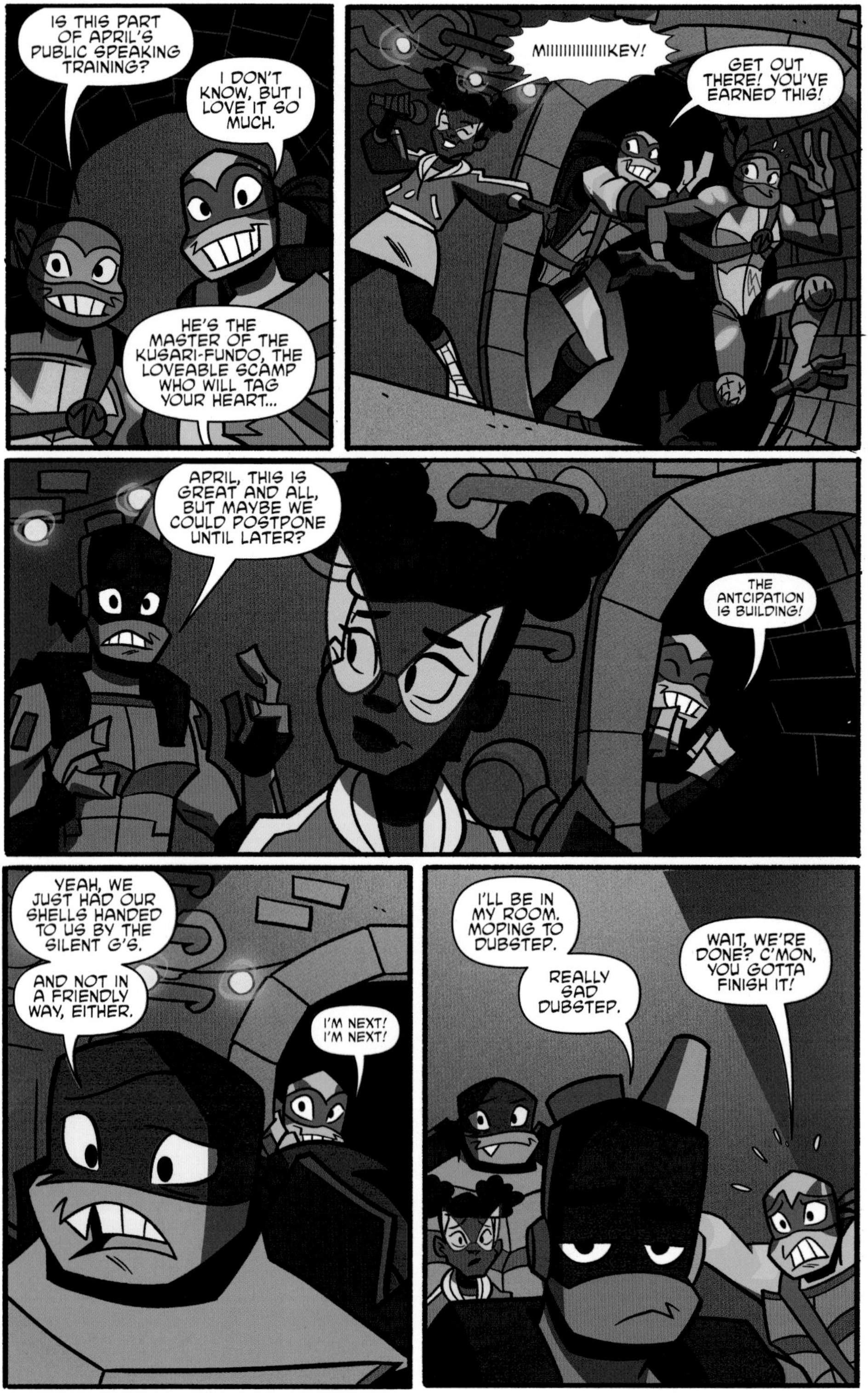
IS THIS PART OF APRIL'S PUBLIC SPEAKING TRAINING?
I DON'T KNOW, BUT I LOVE IT SO MUCH.
HE'S THE MASTER OF THE KUSARI-FUNDO, THE LOVEABLE SCAMP WHO WILL TAG YOUR HEART...
MIIIIIIIIIIIIKEY!
GET OUT THERE! YOU'VE EARNED THIS!
APRIL, THIS IS GREAT AND ALL, BUT MAYBE WE COULD POSTPONE UNTIL LATER?
THE ANTCIPATION IS BUILDING!
YEAH, WE JUST HAD OUR SHELLS HANDED TO US BY THE SILENT G'S.
AND NOT IN A FRIENDLY WAY, EITHER.
I'M NEXT! I'M NEXT!
I'LL BE IN MY ROOM. MOPING TO DUBSTEP.
REALLY SAD DUBSTEP.
WAIT, WE'RE DONE? C'MON, YOU GOTTA FINISH IT!

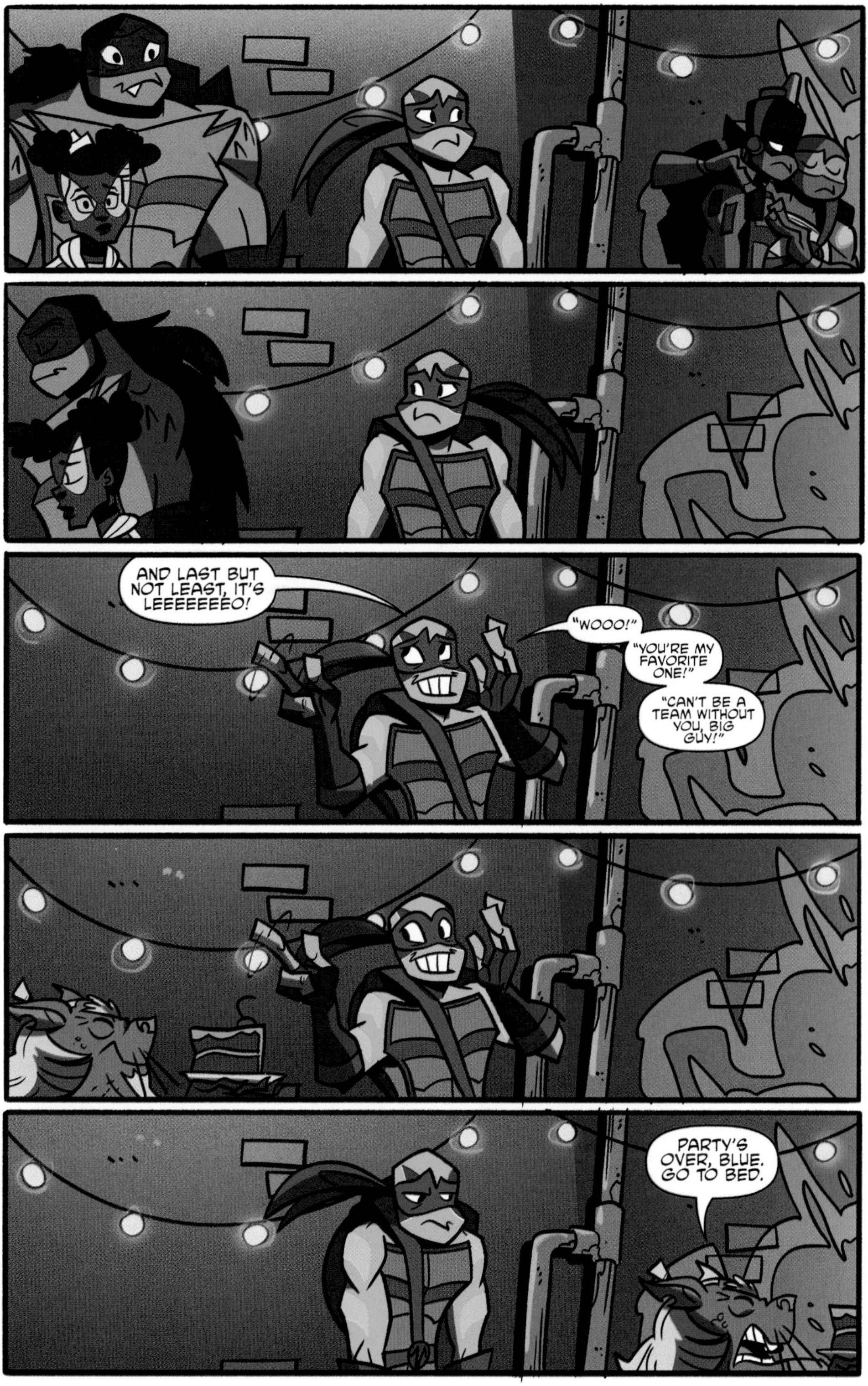
AND LAST BUT NOT LEAST, IT'S LEEEEEEEO!
"WOOO!"
"YOU'RE MY FAVORITE ONE!"
"CAN'T BE A TEAM WITHOUT YOU, BIG GUY!"
PARTY'S OVER, BLUE. GO TO BED.

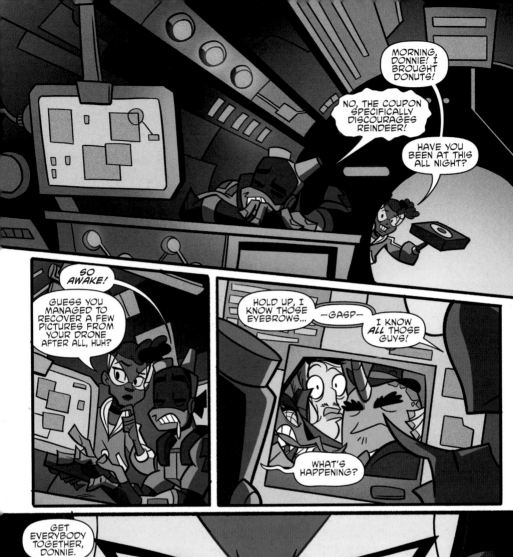

MORNING, DONNIE! I BROUGHT DONUTS!

NO, THE COUPON SPECIFICALLY DISCOURAGES REINDEER!

HAVE YOU BEEN AT THIS ALL NIGHT?

SO AWAKE!

GUESS YOU MANAGED TO RECOVER A FEW PICTURES FROM YOUR DRONE AFTER ALL, HUH?

HOLD UP, I KNOW THOSE EYEBROWS...

—GASP—

I KNOW *ALL* THOSE GUYS!

WHAT'S HAPPENING?

GET EVERYBODY TOGETHER, DONNIE.

IT'S TIME YOU ALL KNOW MY DEEPEST, DARKEST SECRET.

...

WAS SOMEONE JUST HERE?

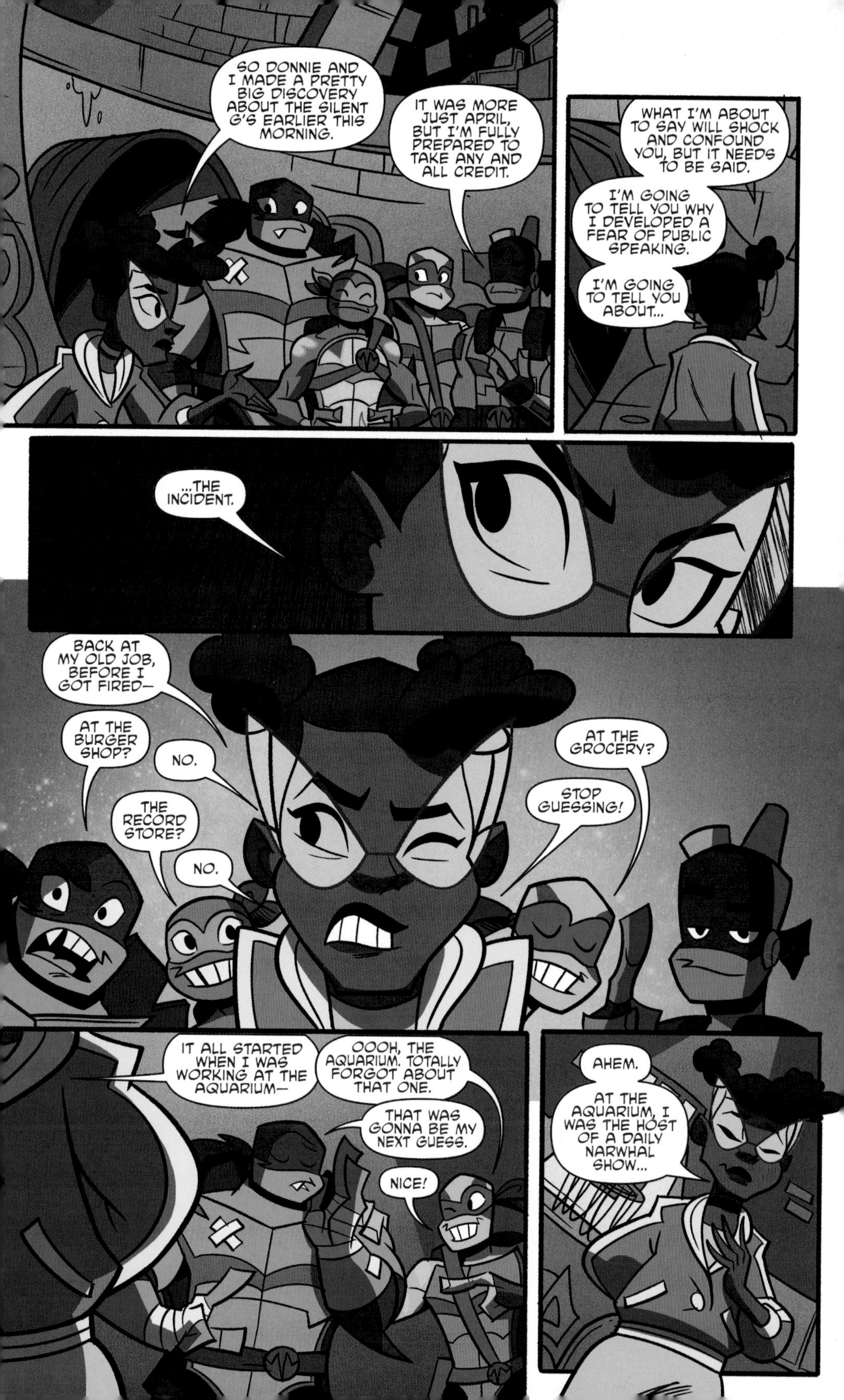

SO DONNIE AND I MADE A PRETTY BIG DISCOVERY ABOUT THE SILENT G'S EARLIER THIS MORNING.
IT WAS MORE JUST APRIL, BUT I'M FULLY PREPARED TO TAKE ANY AND ALL CREDIT.
WHAT I'M ABOUT TO SAY WILL SHOCK AND CONFOUND YOU, BUT IT NEEDS TO BE SAID.
I'M GOING TO TELL YOU WHY I DEVELOPED A FEAR OF PUBLIC SPEAKING.
I'M GOING TO TELL YOU ABOUT...
...THE INCIDENT.
BACK AT MY OLD JOB, BEFORE I GOT FIRED—
AT THE BURGER SHOP?
NO.
THE RECORD STORE?
NO.
AT THE GROCERY?
STOP GUESSING!
IT ALL STARTED WHEN I WAS WORKING AT THE AQUARIUM—
OOOH, THE AQUARIUM. TOTALLY FORGOT ABOUT THAT ONE.
THAT WAS GONNA BE MY NEXT GUESS.
NICE!
AHEM.
AT THE AQUARIUM, I WAS THE HOST OF A DAILY NARWHAL SHOW...

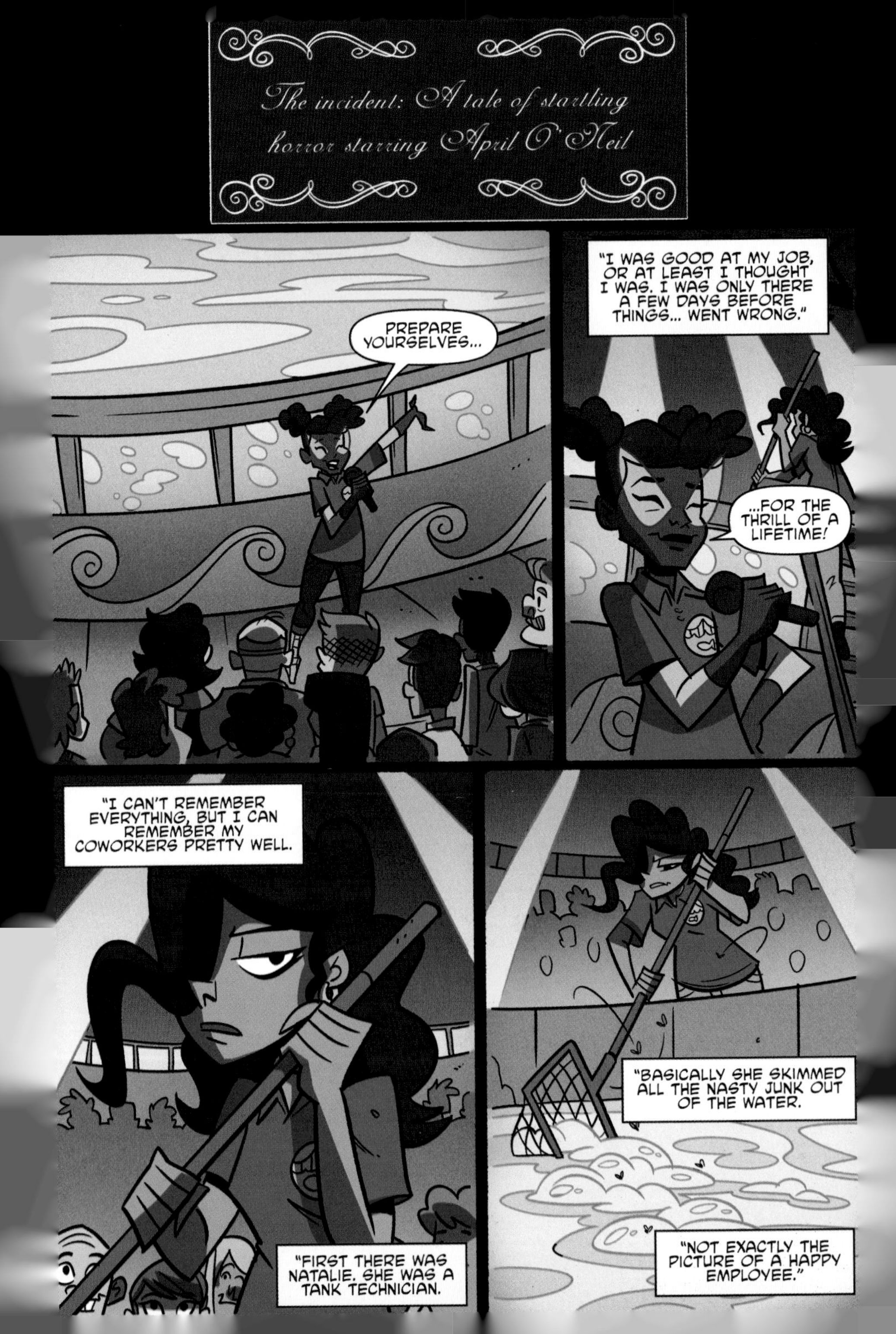
The incident: A tale of startling horror starring April O'Neil
PREPARE YOURSELVES...
"I WAS GOOD AT MY JOB, OR AT LEAST I THOUGHT I WAS. I WAS ONLY THERE A FEW DAYS BEFORE THINGS... WENT WRONG."
...FOR THE THRILL OF A LIFETIME!
"I CAN'T REMEMBER EVERYTHING, BUT I CAN REMEMBER MY COWORKERS PRETTY WELL.
"FIRST THERE WAS NATALIE. SHE WAS A TANK TECHNICIAN.
"BASICALLY SHE SKIMMED ALL THE NASTY JUNK OUT OF THE WATER.
"NOT EXACTLY THE PICTURE OF A HAPPY EMPLOYEE."

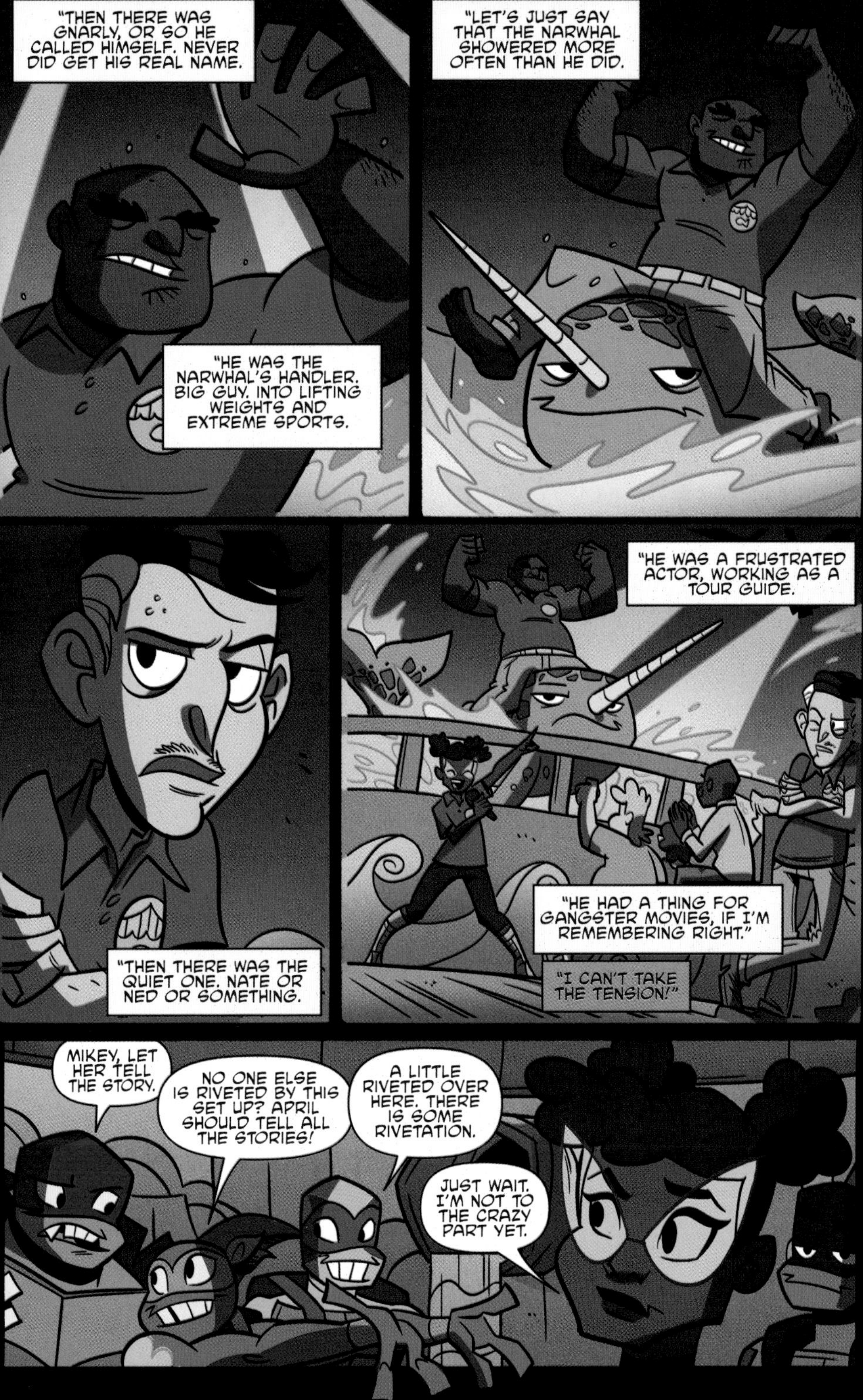
"THEN THERE WAS GNARLY, OR SO HE CALLED HIMSELF. NEVER DID GET HIS REAL NAME.
"HE WAS THE NARWHAL'S HANDLER. BIG GUY. INTO LIFTING WEIGHTS AND EXTREME SPORTS.
"LET'S JUST SAY THAT THE NARWHAL SHOWERED MORE OFTEN THAN HE DID.
"THEN THERE WAS THE QUIET ONE. NATE OR NED OR SOMETHING.
"HE WAS A FRUSTRATED ACTOR, WORKING AS A TOUR GUIDE.
"HE HAD A THING FOR GANGSTER MOVIES, IF I'M REMEMBERING RIGHT."
"I CAN'T TAKE THE TENSION!"
MIKEY, LET HER TELL THE STORY.
NO ONE ELSE IS RIVETED BY THIS SET UP? APRIL SHOULD TELL ALL THE STORIES!
A LITTLE RIVETED OVER HERE. THERE IS SOME RIVETATION.
JUST WAIT. I'M NOT TO THE CRAZY PART YET.

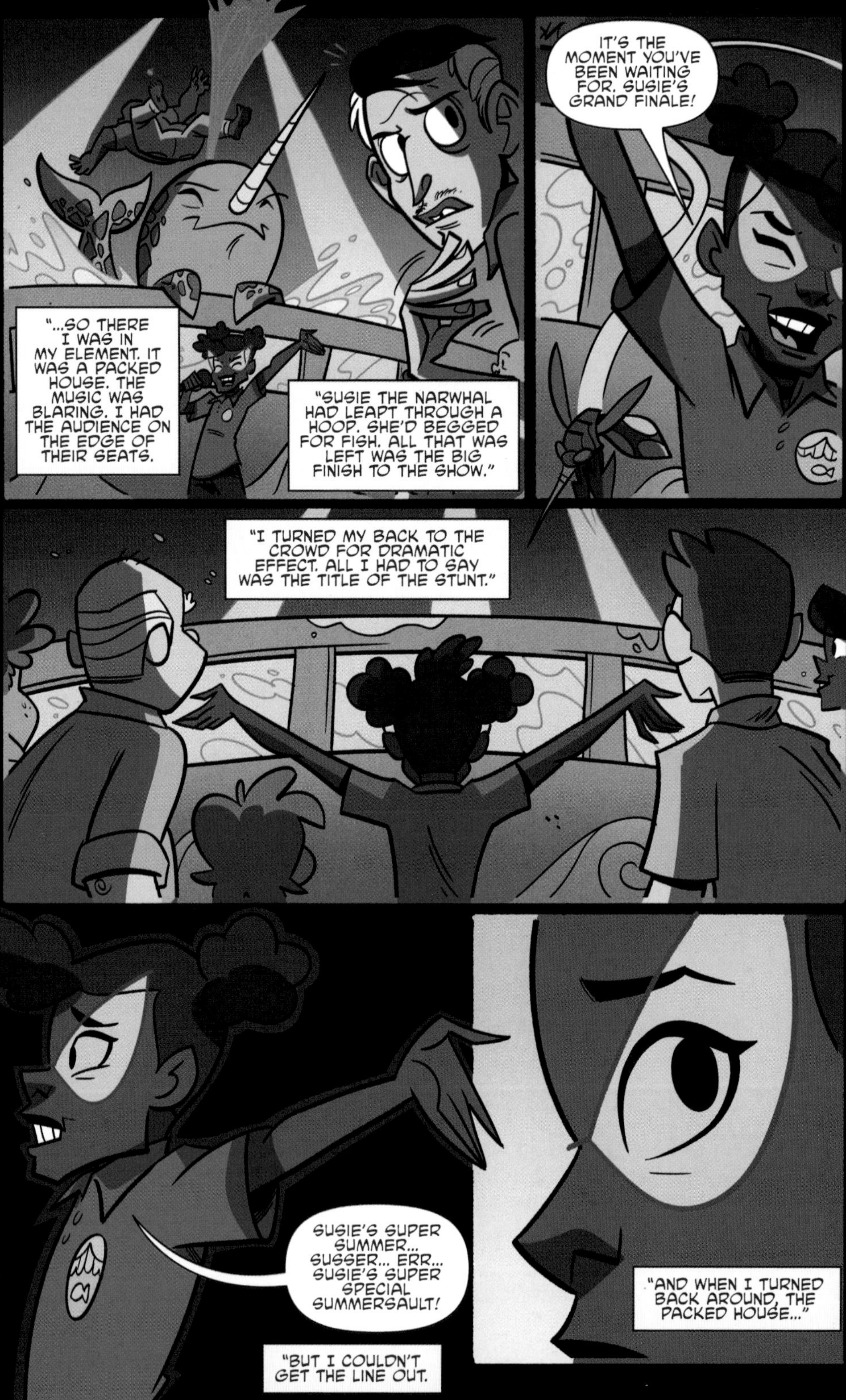
"...SO THERE I WAS IN MY ELEMENT. IT WAS A PACKED HOUSE. THE MUSIC WAS BLARING. I HAD THE AUDIENCE ON THE EDGE OF THEIR SEATS.
"SUSIE THE NARWHAL HAD LEAPT THROUGH A HOOP. SHE'D BEGGED FOR FISH. ALL THAT WAS LEFT WAS THE BIG FINISH TO THE SHOW."
IT'S THE MOMENT YOU'VE BEEN WAITING FOR. SUSIE'S GRAND FINALE!
"I TURNED MY BACK TO THE CROWD FOR DRAMATIC EFFECT. ALL I HAD TO SAY WAS THE TITLE OF THE STUNT."
SUSIE'S SUPER SUMMER... SUSSER... ERR... SUSIE'S SUPER SPECIAL SUMMERSAULT!
"BUT I COULDN'T GET THE LINE OUT.
"AND WHEN I TURNED BACK AROUND, THE PACKED HOUSE..."

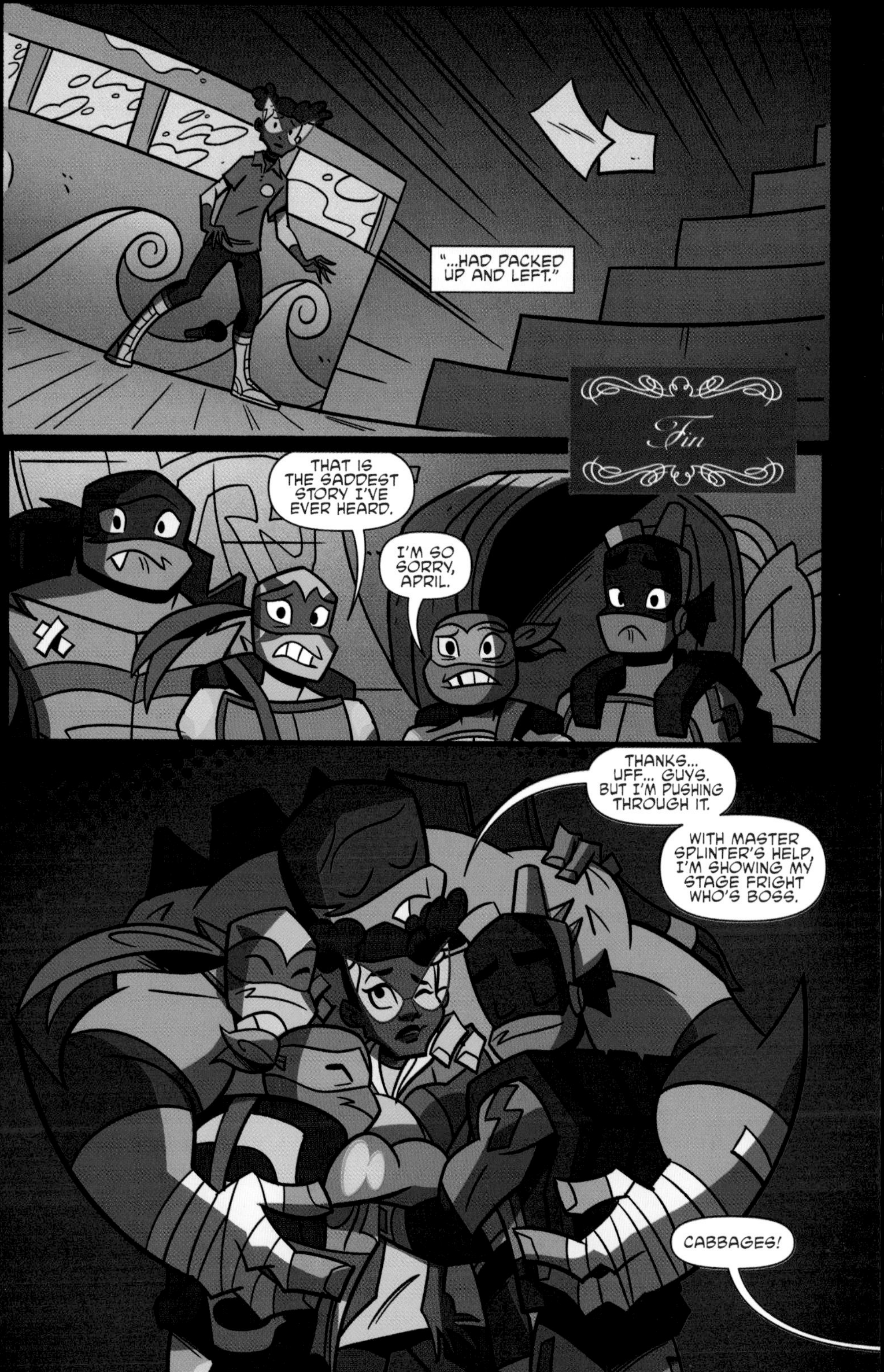
"...HAD PACKED UP AND LEFT."
Fin
THAT IS THE SADDEST STORY I'VE EVER HEARD.
I'M SO SORRY, APRIL.
THANKS... UFF... GUYS. BUT I'M PUSHING THROUGH IT.
WITH MASTER SPLINTER'S HELP, I'M SHOWING MY STAGE FRIGHT WHO'S BOSS.
CABBAGES!

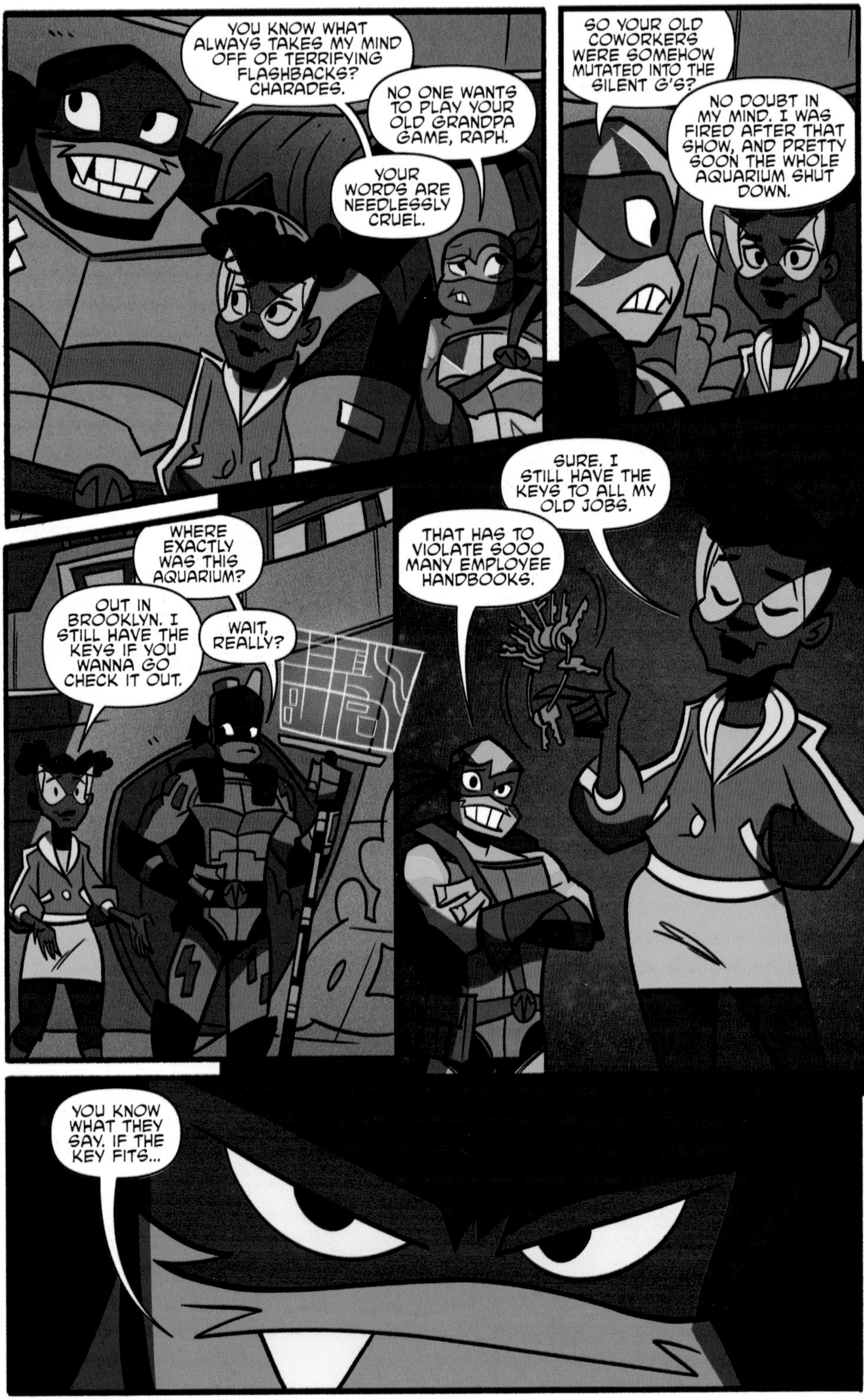
YOU KNOW WHAT ALWAYS TAKES MY MIND OFF OF TERRIFYING FLASHBACKS? CHARADES.
NO ONE WANTS TO PLAY YOUR OLD GRANDPA GAME, RAPH.
YOUR WORDS ARE NEEDLESSLY CRUEL.
SO YOUR OLD COWORKERS WERE SOMEHOW MUTATED INTO THE SILENT G'S?
NO DOUBT IN MY MIND. I WAS FIRED AFTER THAT SHOW, AND PRETTY SOON THE WHOLE AQUARIUM SHUT DOWN.
WHERE EXACTLY WAS THIS AQUARIUM?
OUT IN BROOKLYN. I STILL HAVE THE KEYS IF YOU WANNA GO CHECK IT OUT.
WAIT, REALLY?
SURE. I STILL HAVE THE KEYS TO ALL MY OLD JOBS.
THAT HAS TO VIOLATE SOOO MANY EMPLOYEE HANDBOOKS.
YOU KNOW WHAT THEY SAY. IF THE KEY FITS...

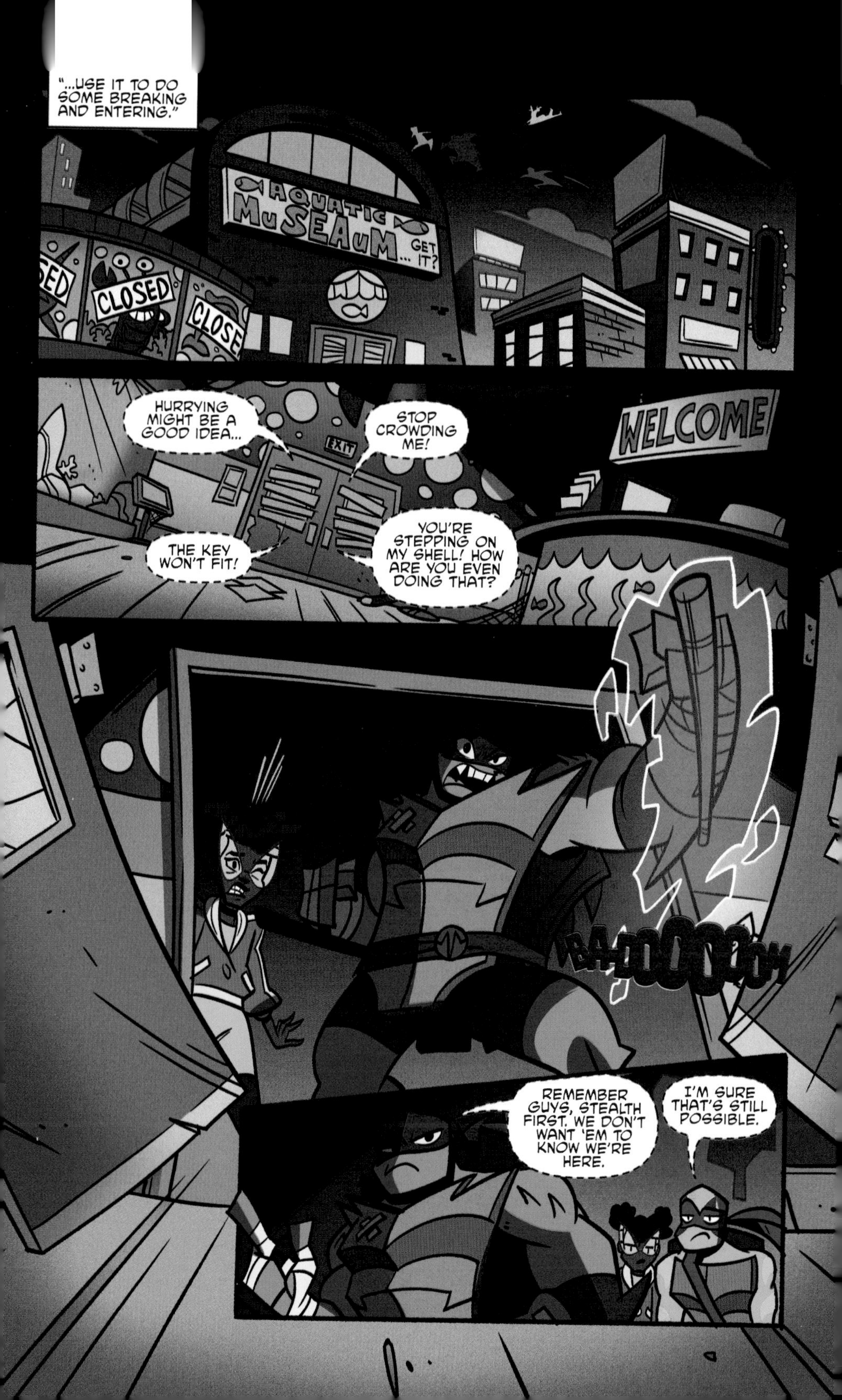
"...USE IT TO DO SOME BREAKING AND ENTERING."
AQUATIC MuSEAuM... GET IT?
CLOSED
CLOSE
HURRYING MIGHT BE A GOOD IDEA...
STOP CROWDING ME!
EXIT
WELCOME
THE KEY WON'T FIT!
YOU'RE STEPPING ON MY SHELL! HOW ARE YOU EVEN DOING THAT?
BADOOOOOOM
REMEMBER GUYS, STEALTH FIRST. WE DON'T WANT 'EM TO KNOW WE'RE HERE.
I'M SURE THAT'S STILL POSSIBLE.

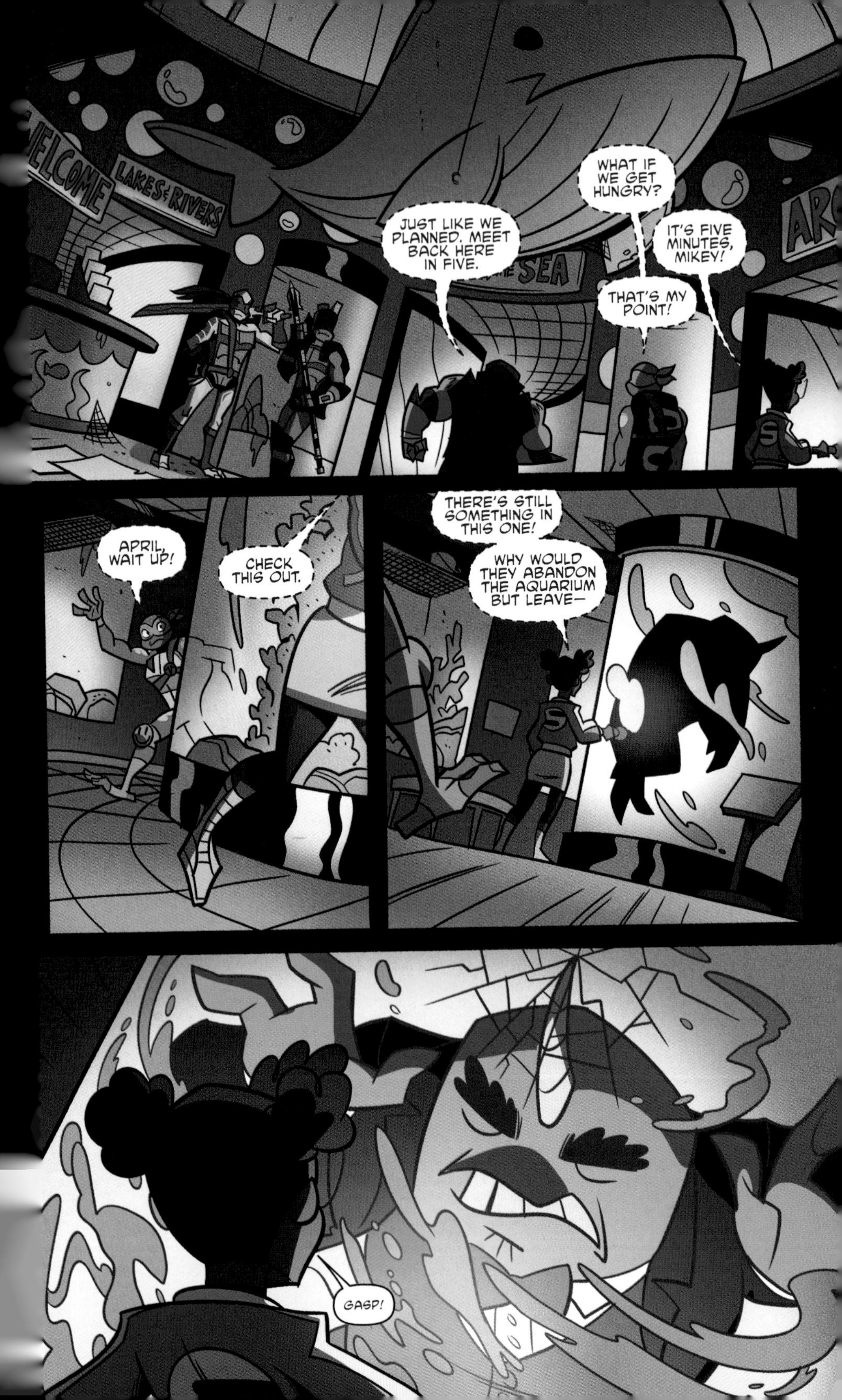
WELCOME
LAKES & RIVERS
SEA
JUST LIKE WE PLANNED. MEET BACK HERE IN FIVE.
WHAT IF WE GET HUNGRY?
IT'S FIVE MINUTES, MIKEY!
THAT'S MY POINT!
APRIL, WAIT UP!
CHECK THIS OUT.
THERE'S STILL SOMETHING IN THIS ONE!
WHY WOULD THEY ABANDON THE AQUARIUM BUT LEAVE—
GASP!

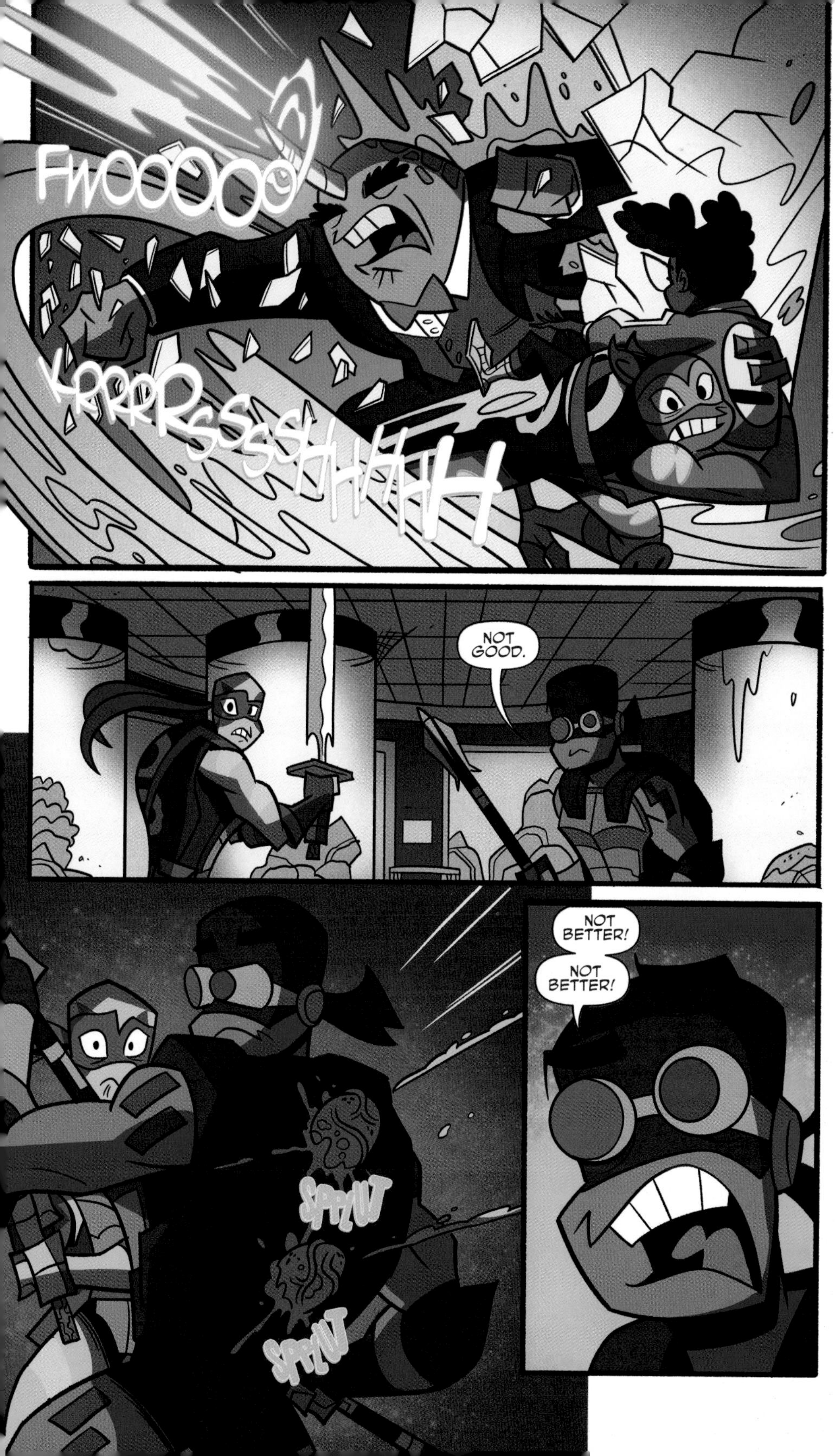
FWOOOOOO
KRRRRRSSSSSHHHHHH
NOT GOOD.
SPPLUT
SPPLUT
NOT BETTER!
NOT BETTER!

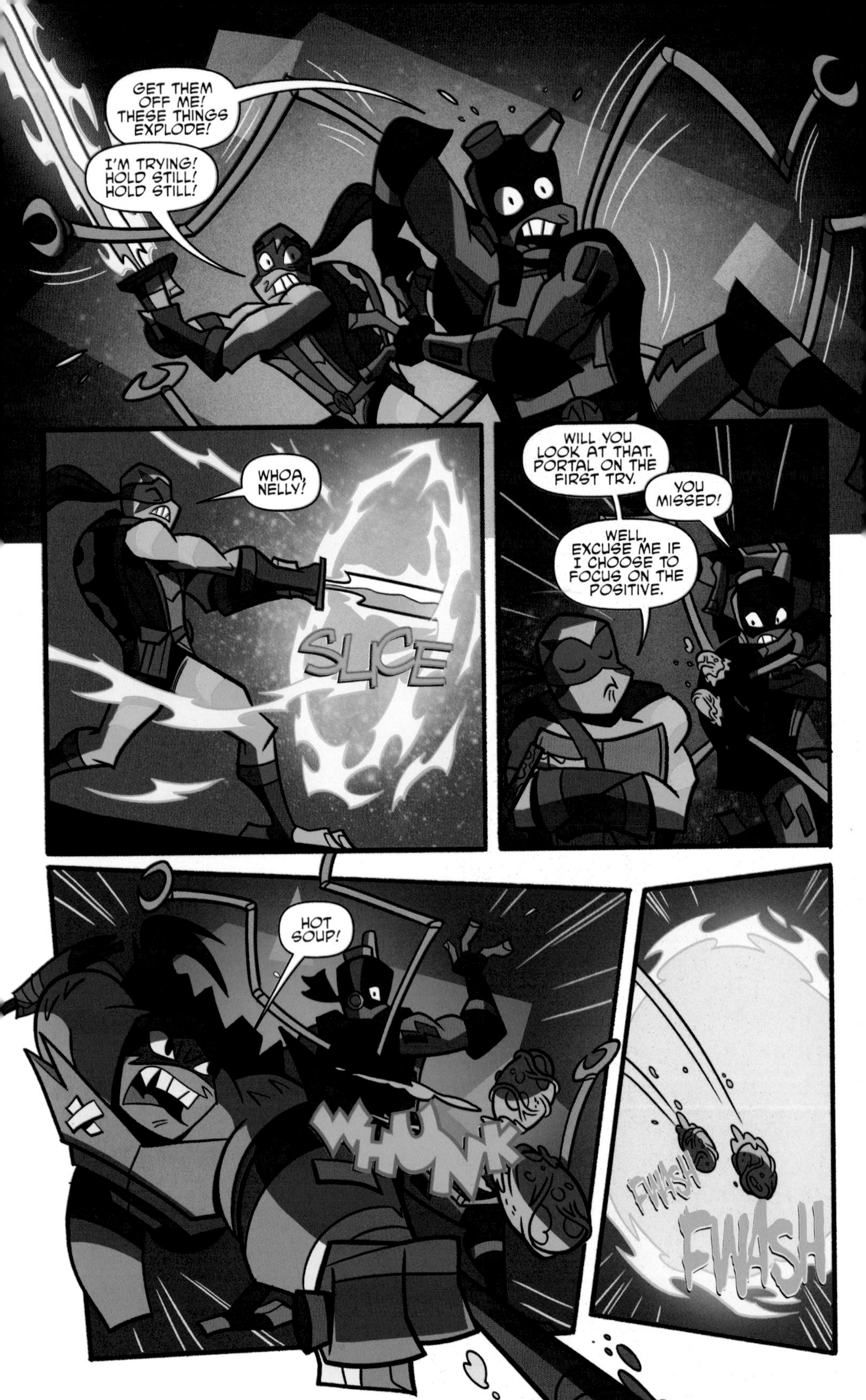
GET THEM OFF ME! THESE THINGS EXPLODE!
I'M TRYING! HOLD STILL! HOLD STILL!
WHOA, NELLY!
SLICE
WILL YOU LOOK AT THAT. PORTAL ON THE FIRST TRY.
YOU MISSED!
WELL, EXCUSE ME IF I CHOOSE TO FOCUS ON THE POSITIVE.
HOT SOUP!
WHUNK
FWASH
FWASH

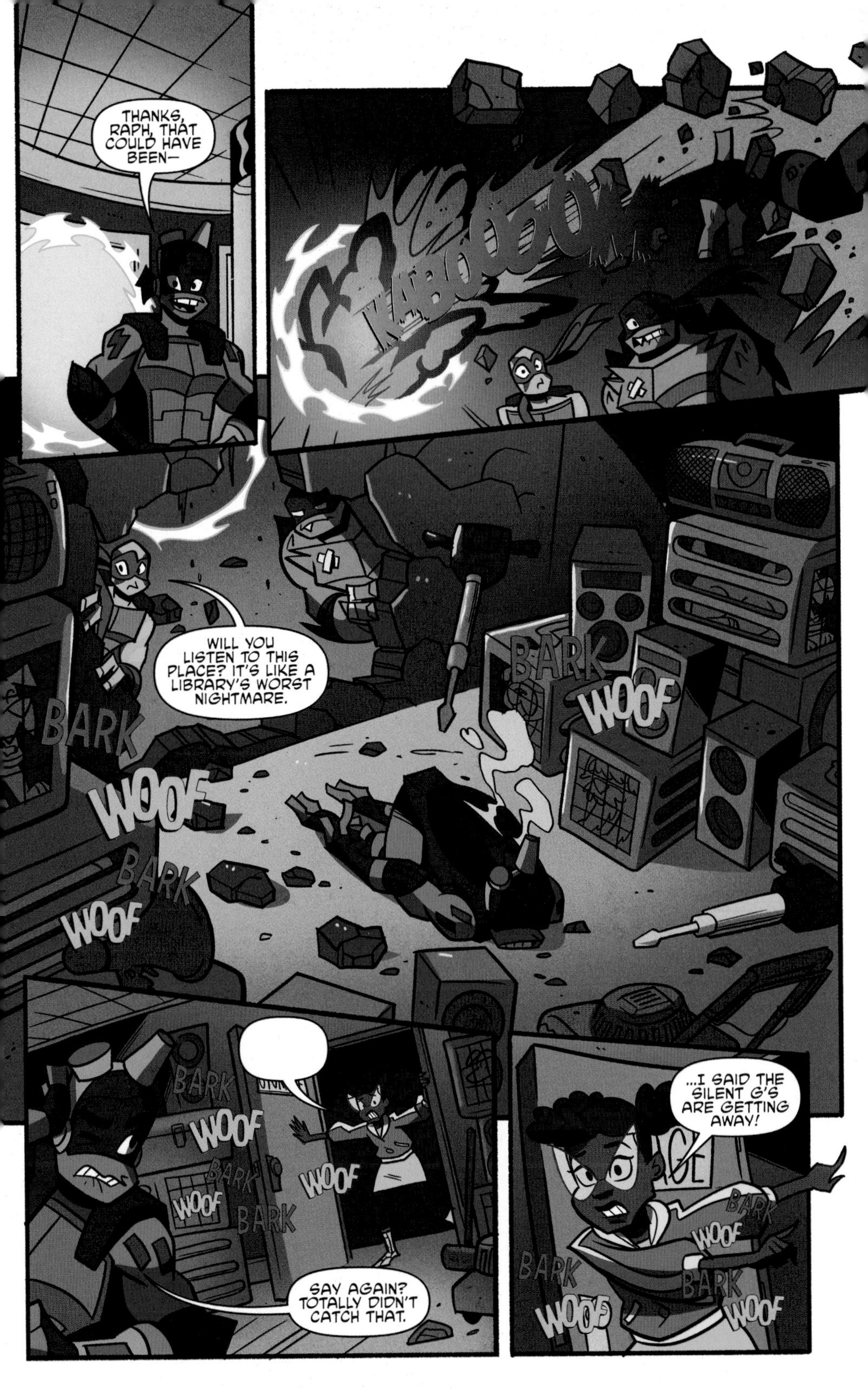
THANKS, RAPH, THAT COULD HAVE BEEN—
KABOOOOOM
WILL YOU LISTEN TO THIS PLACE? IT'S LIKE A LIBRARY'S WORST NIGHTMARE.
BARK
WOOF
BARK
WOOF
BARK
WOOF
BARK
WOOF
BARK
WOOF
BARK
WOOF
SAY AGAIN? TOTALLY DIDN'T CATCH THAT.
...I SAID THE SILENT G'S ARE GETTING AWAY!
BARK
WOOF
BARK
WOOF
BARK
WOOF

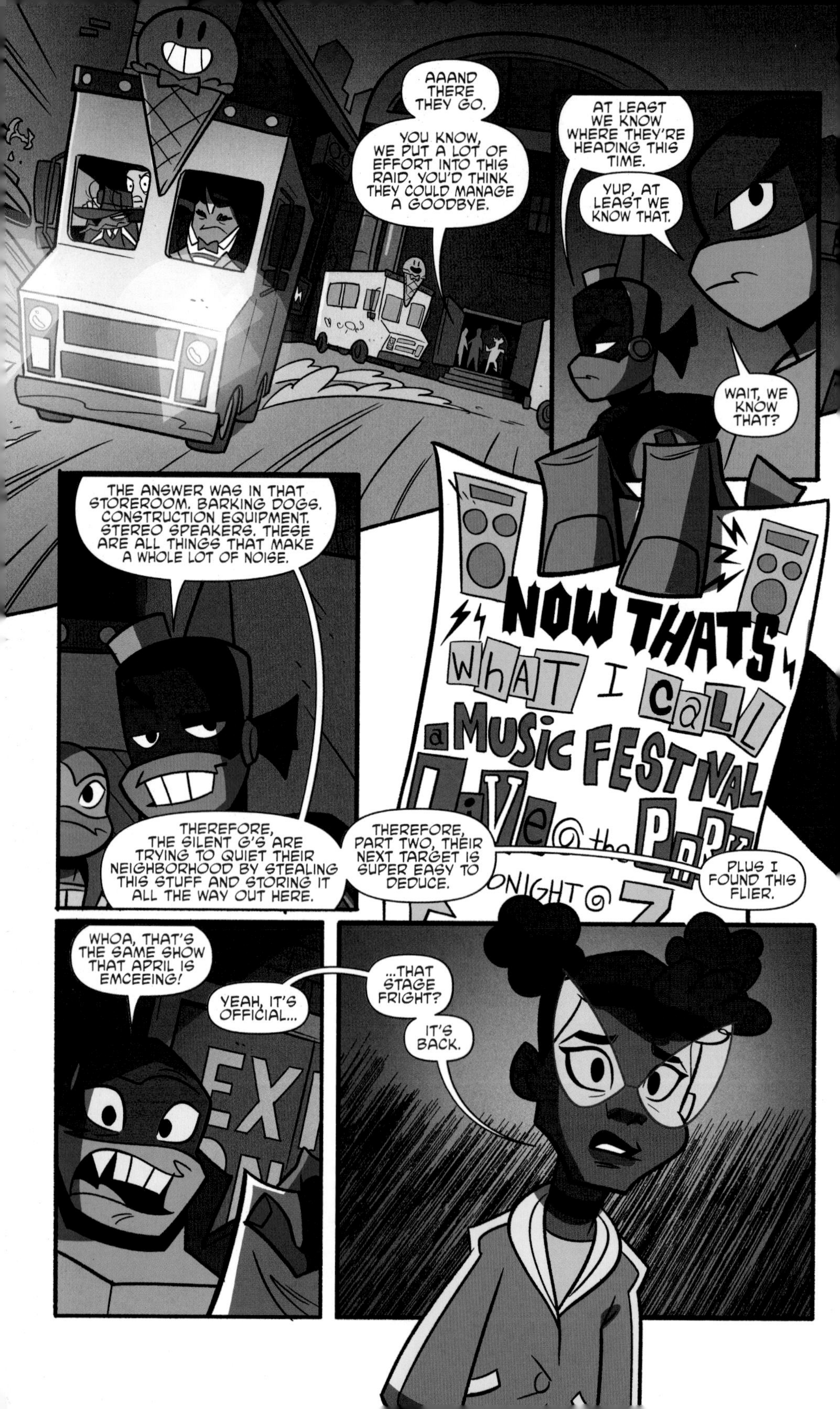

AAAND THERE THEY GO.
YOU KNOW, WE PUT A LOT OF EFFORT INTO THIS RAID. YOU'D THINK THEY COULD MANAGE A GOODBYE.
AT LEAST WE KNOW WHERE THEY'RE HEADING THIS TIME.
YUP, AT LEAST WE KNOW THAT.
WAIT, WE KNOW THAT?
THE ANSWER WAS IN THAT STOREROOM. BARKING DOGS. CONSTRUCTION EQUIPMENT. STEREO SPEAKERS. THESE ARE ALL THINGS THAT MAKE A WHOLE LOT OF NOISE.
NOW THATS WHAT I CALL A MUSIC FESTIVAL
THEREFORE, THE SILENT G'S ARE TRYING TO QUIET THEIR NEIGHBORHOOD BY STEALING THIS STUFF AND STORING IT ALL THE WAY OUT HERE.
THEREFORE, PART TWO, THEIR NEXT TARGET IS SUPER EASY TO DEDUCE.
PLUS I FOUND THIS FLIER.
WHOA, THAT'S THE SAME SHOW THAT APRIL IS EMCEEING!
YEAH, IT'S OFFICIAL...
...THAT STAGE FRIGHT?
IT'S BACK.

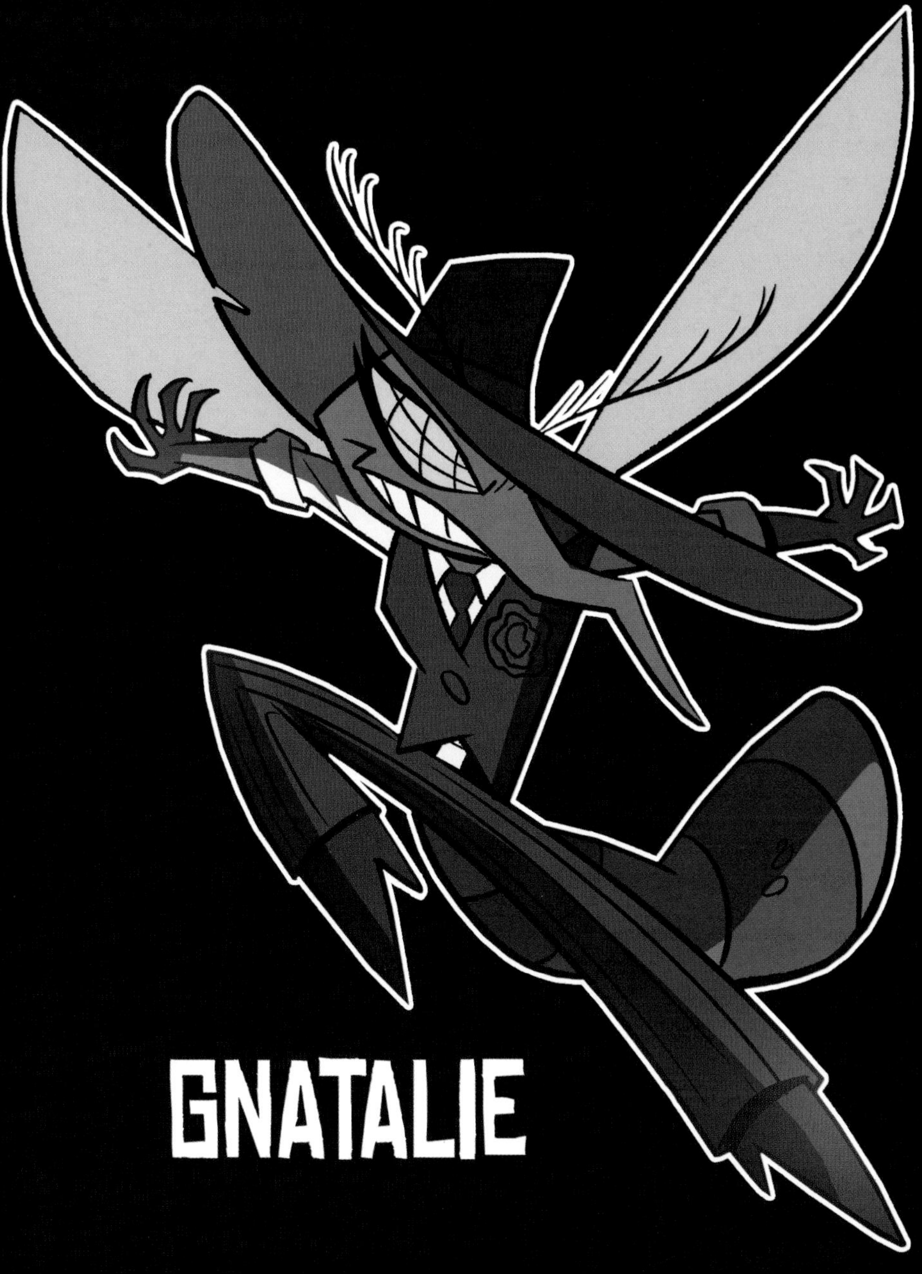
GNATALIE

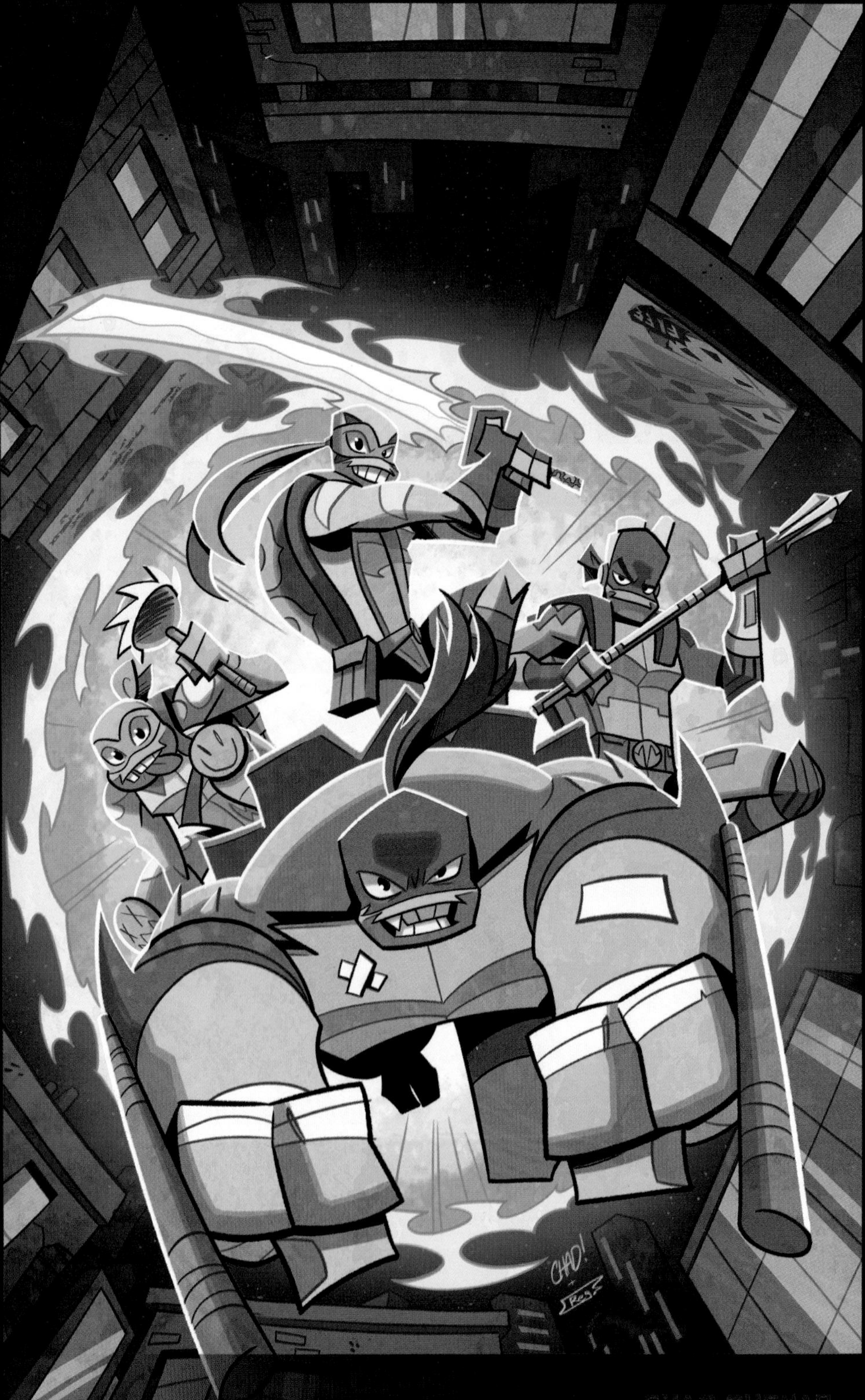

ART BY CHAD THOMAS

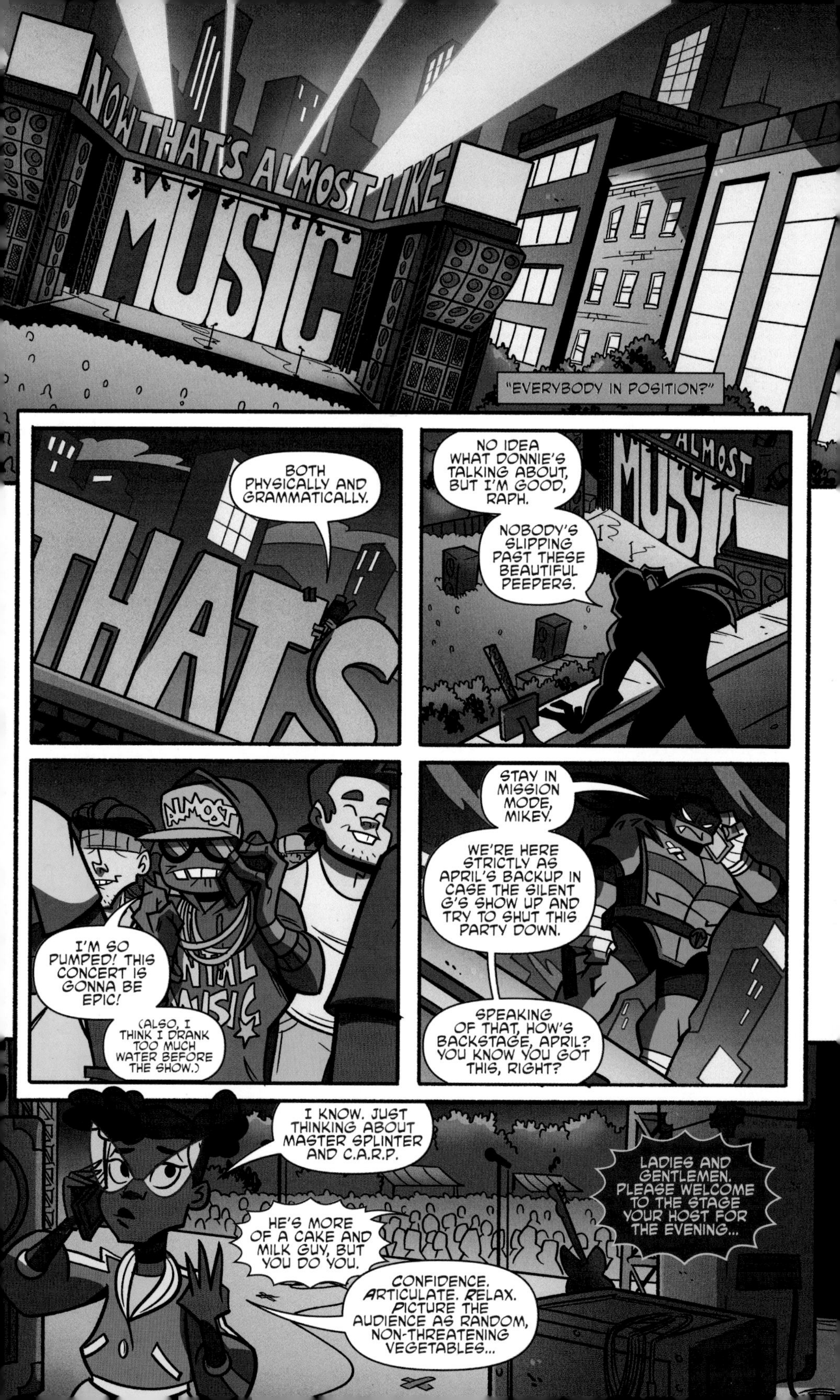
NOW THAT'S ALMOST LIKE MUSIC
"EVERYBODY IN POSITION?"
BOTH PHYSICALLY AND GRAMMATICALLY.
NO IDEA WHAT DONNIE'S TALKING ABOUT, BUT I'M GOOD, RAPH.
NOBODY'S SLIPPING PAST THESE BEAUTIFUL PEEPERS.
ALMOST
I'M SO PUMPED! THIS CONCERT IS GONNA BE EPIC!
(ALSO, I THINK I DRANK TOO MUCH WATER BEFORE THE SHOW.)
STAY IN MISSION MODE, MIKEY.
WE'RE HERE STRICTLY AS APRIL'S BACKUP IN CASE THE SILENT G'S SHOW UP AND TRY TO SHUT THIS PARTY DOWN.
SPEAKING OF THAT, HOW'S BACKSTAGE, APRIL? YOU KNOW YOU GOT THIS, RIGHT?
I KNOW. JUST THINKING ABOUT MASTER SPLINTER AND C.A.R.P.
HE'S MORE OF A CAKE AND MILK GUY, BUT YOU DO YOU.
CONFIDENCE. ARTICULATE. RELAX. PICTURE THE AUDIENCE AS RANDOM, NON-THREATENING VEGETABLES...
LADIES AND GENTLEMEN. PLEASE WELCOME TO THE STAGE YOUR HOST FOR THE EVENING...

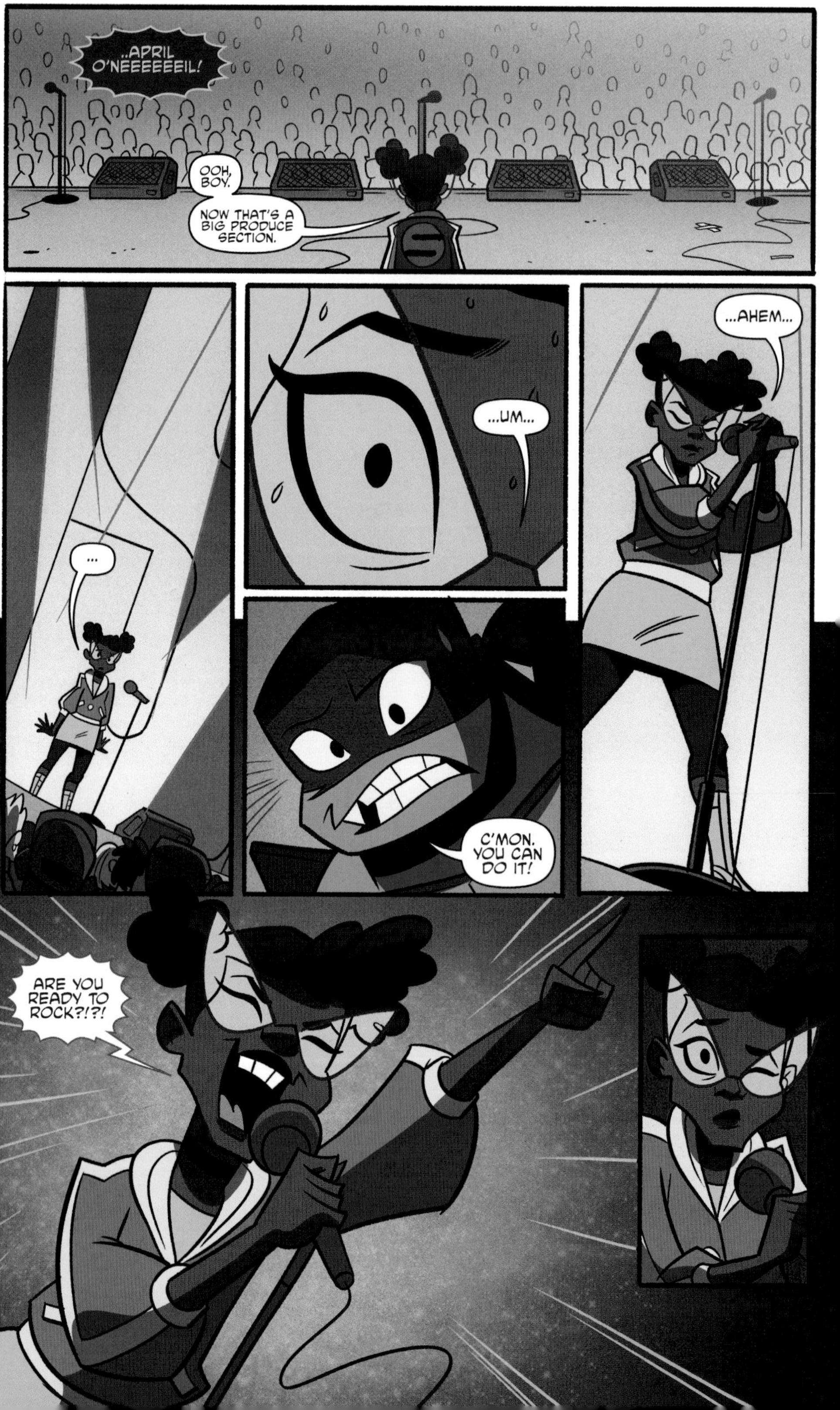
..APRIL O'NEEEEEEIL!
OOH, BOY.
NOW THAT'S A BIG PRODUCE SECTION.
...
...UM...
C'MON. YOU CAN DO IT!
...AHEM...
ARE YOU READY TO ROCK?!?!

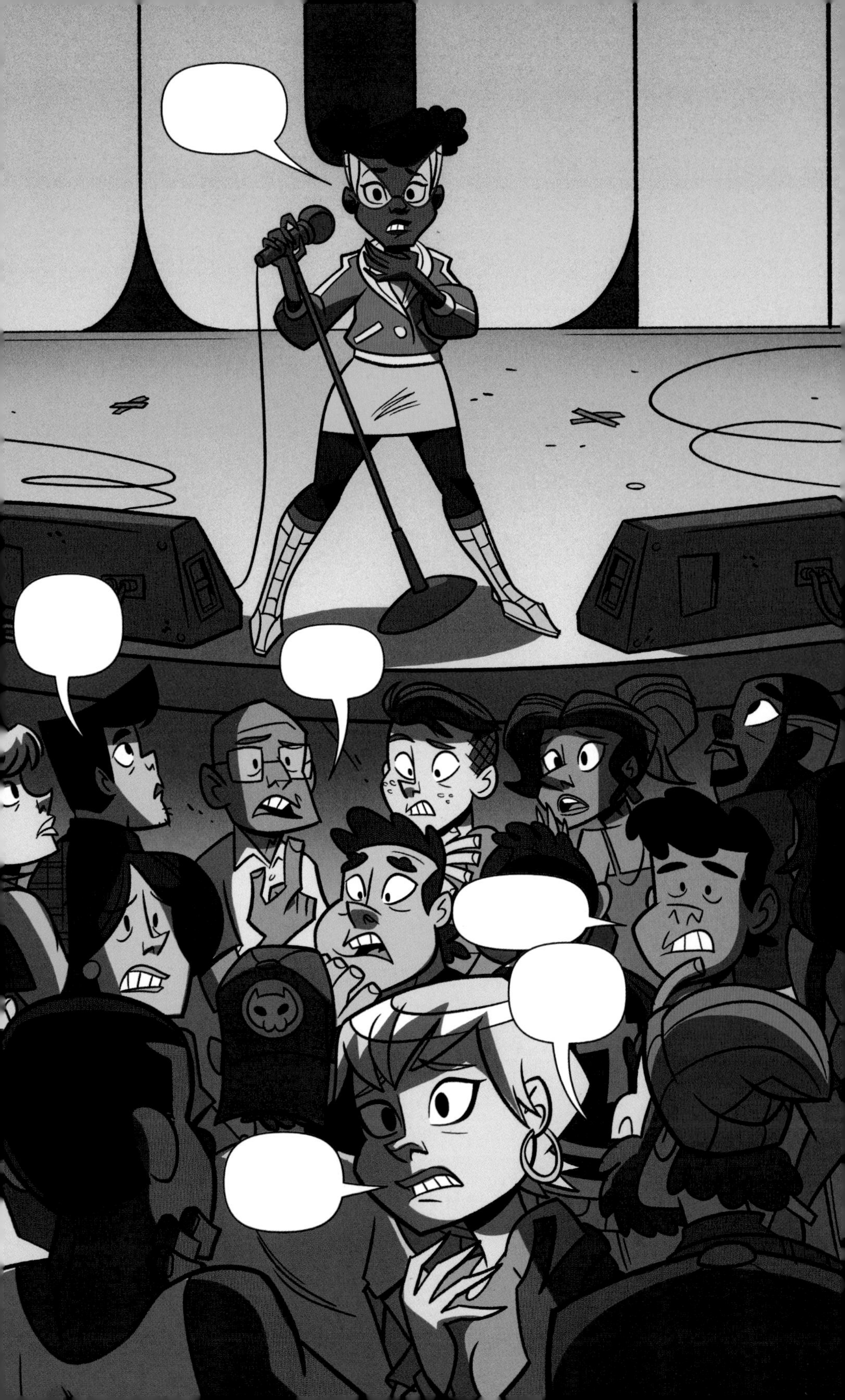

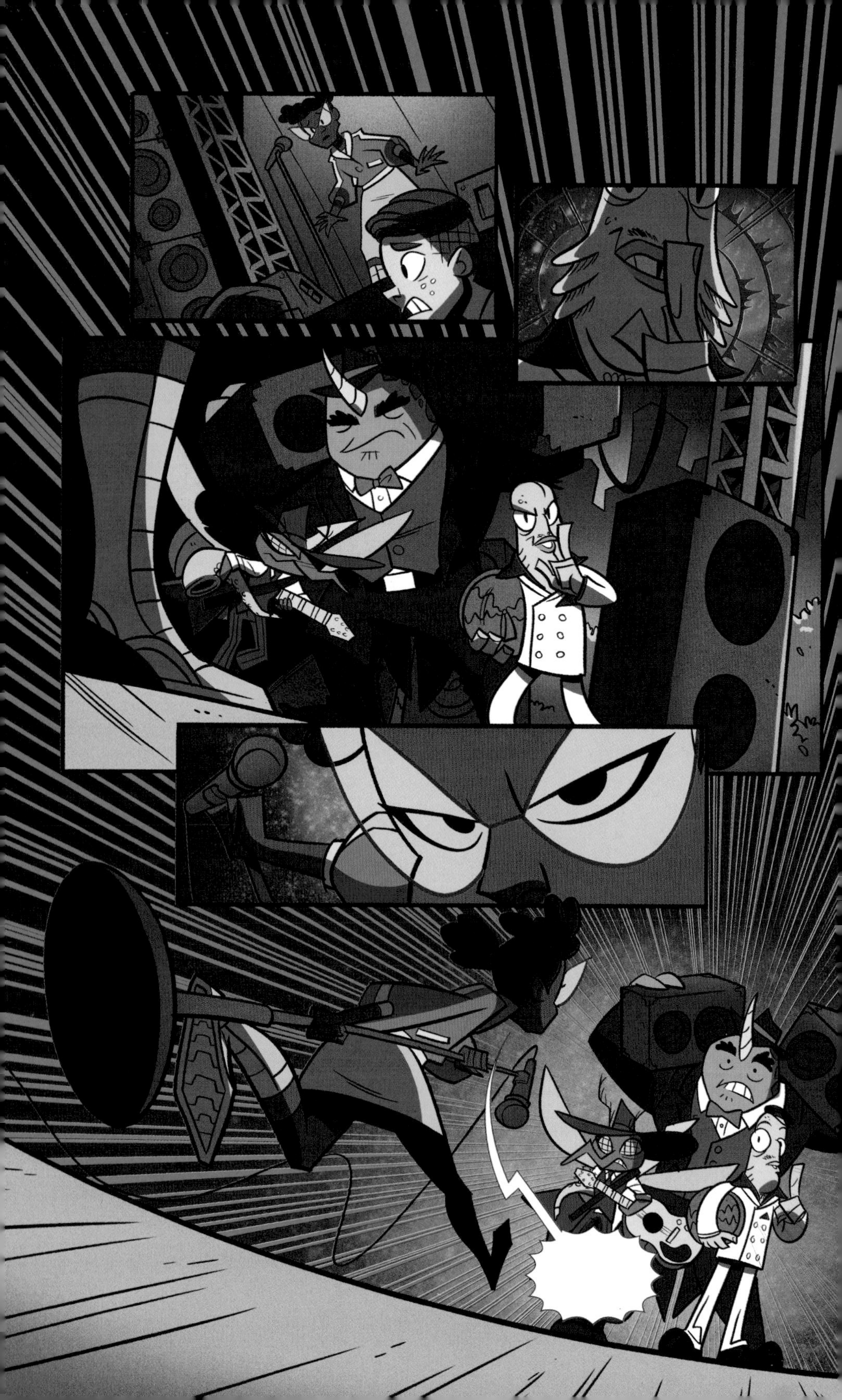

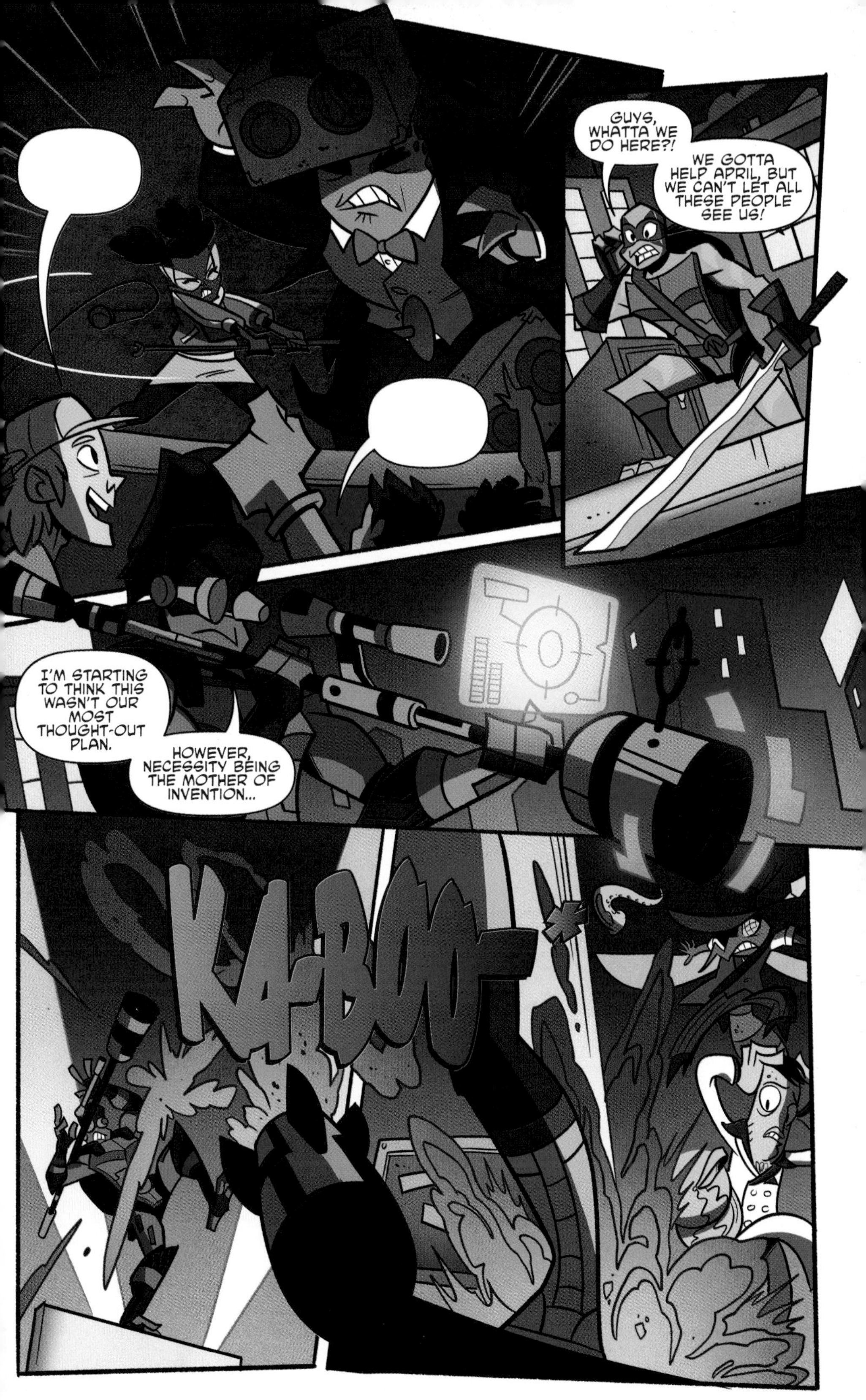
GUYS, WHATTA WE DO HERE?!
WE GOTTA HELP APRIL, BUT WE CAN'T LET ALL THESE PEOPLE SEE US!
I'M STARTING TO THINK THIS WASN'T OUR MOST THOUGHT-OUT PLAN.
HOWEVER, NECESSITY BEING THE MOTHER OF INVENTION...
KA-BOOM

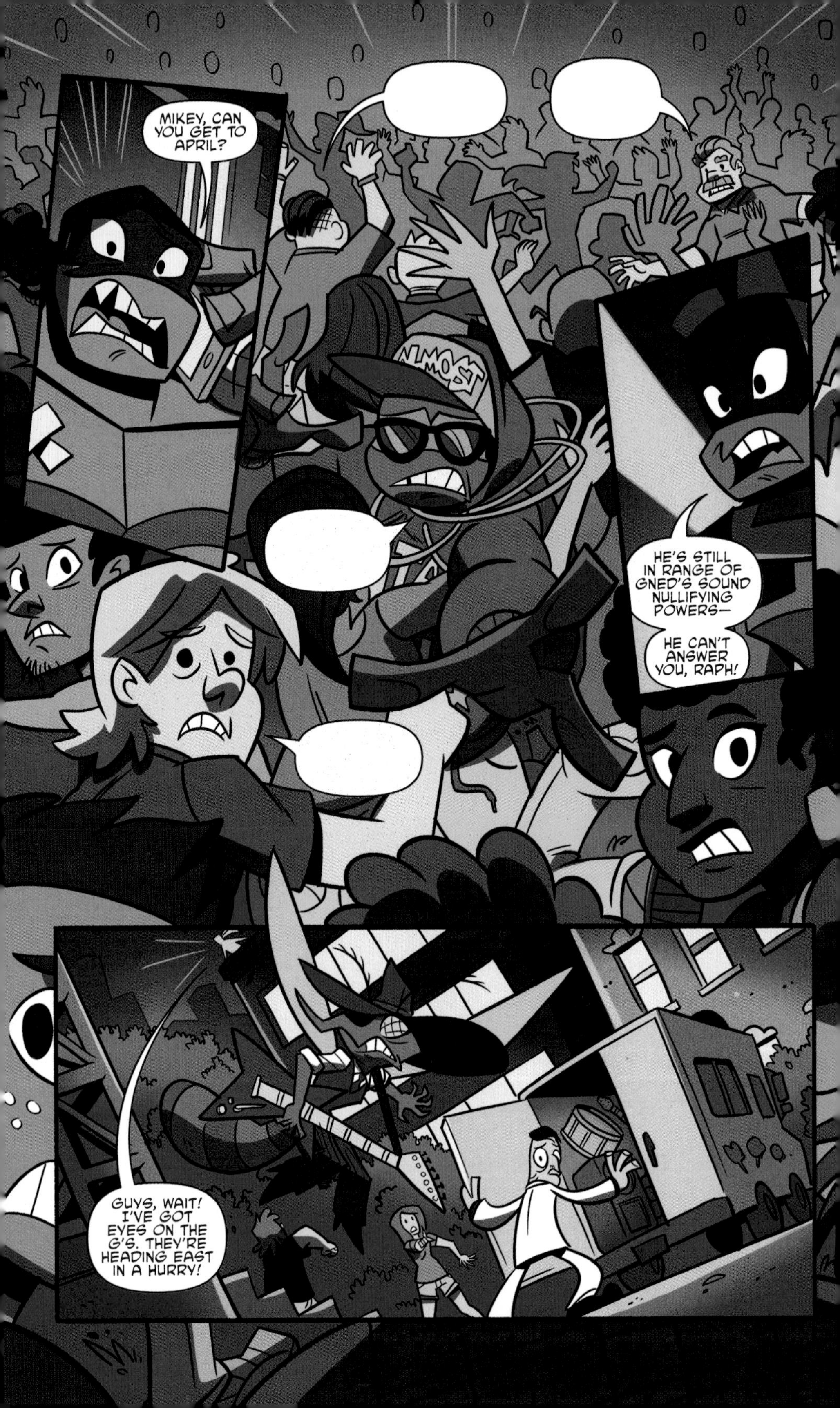
MIKEY, CAN YOU GET TO APRIL?
HE'S STILL IN RANGE OF GNED'S SOUND NULLIFYING POWERS—
HE CAN'T ANSWER YOU, RAPH!
GUYS, WAIT! I'VE GOT EYES ON THE G'S. THEY'RE HEADING EAST IN A HURRY!
ALMOST

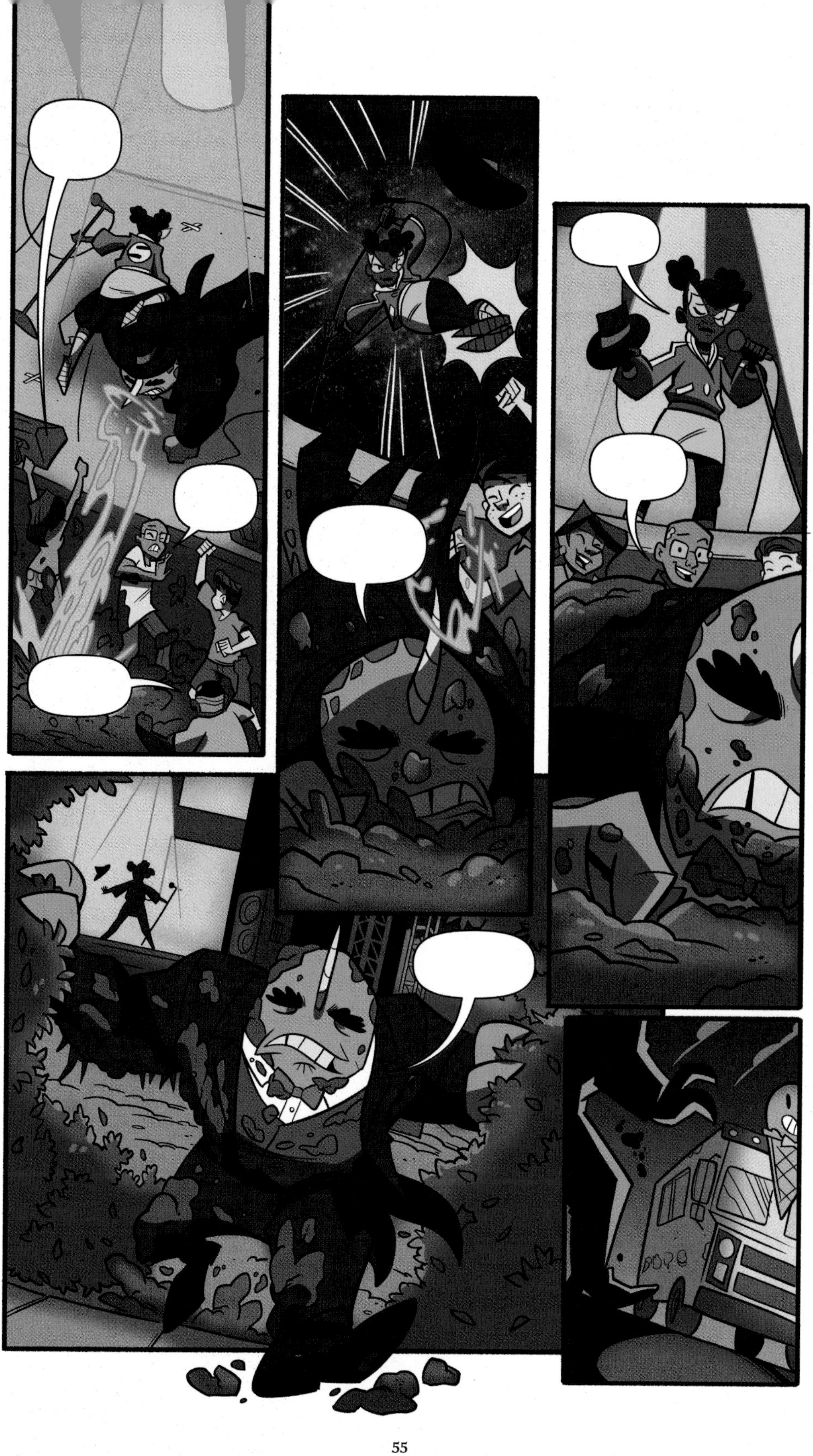

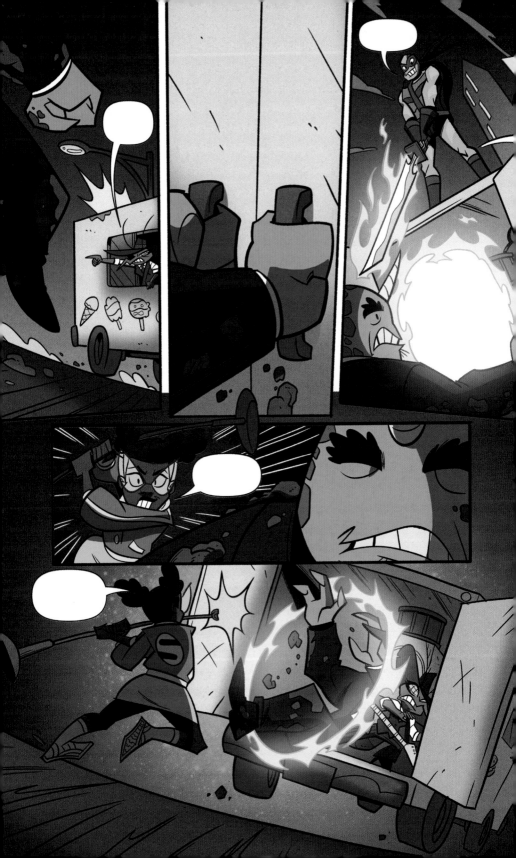

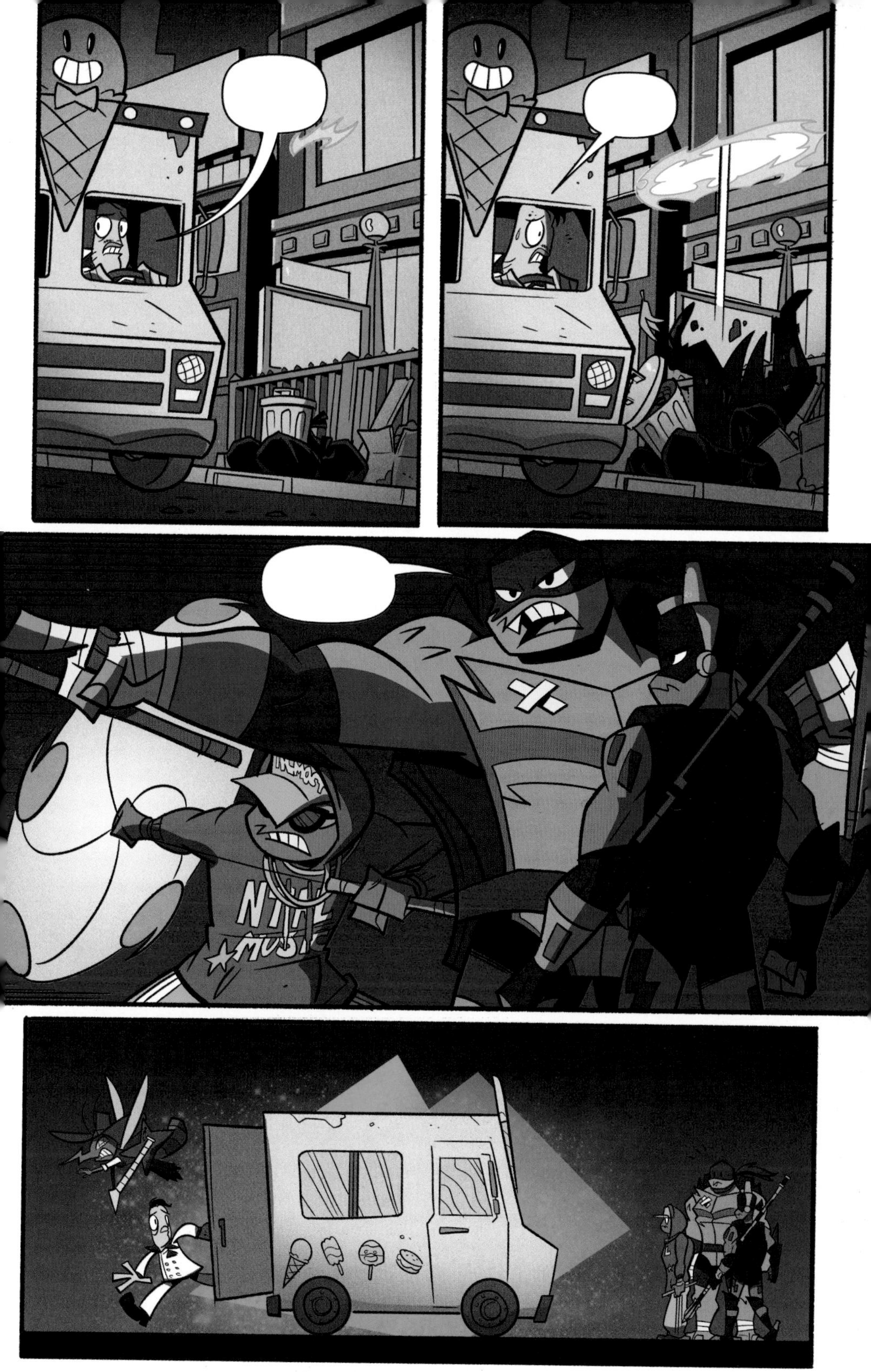

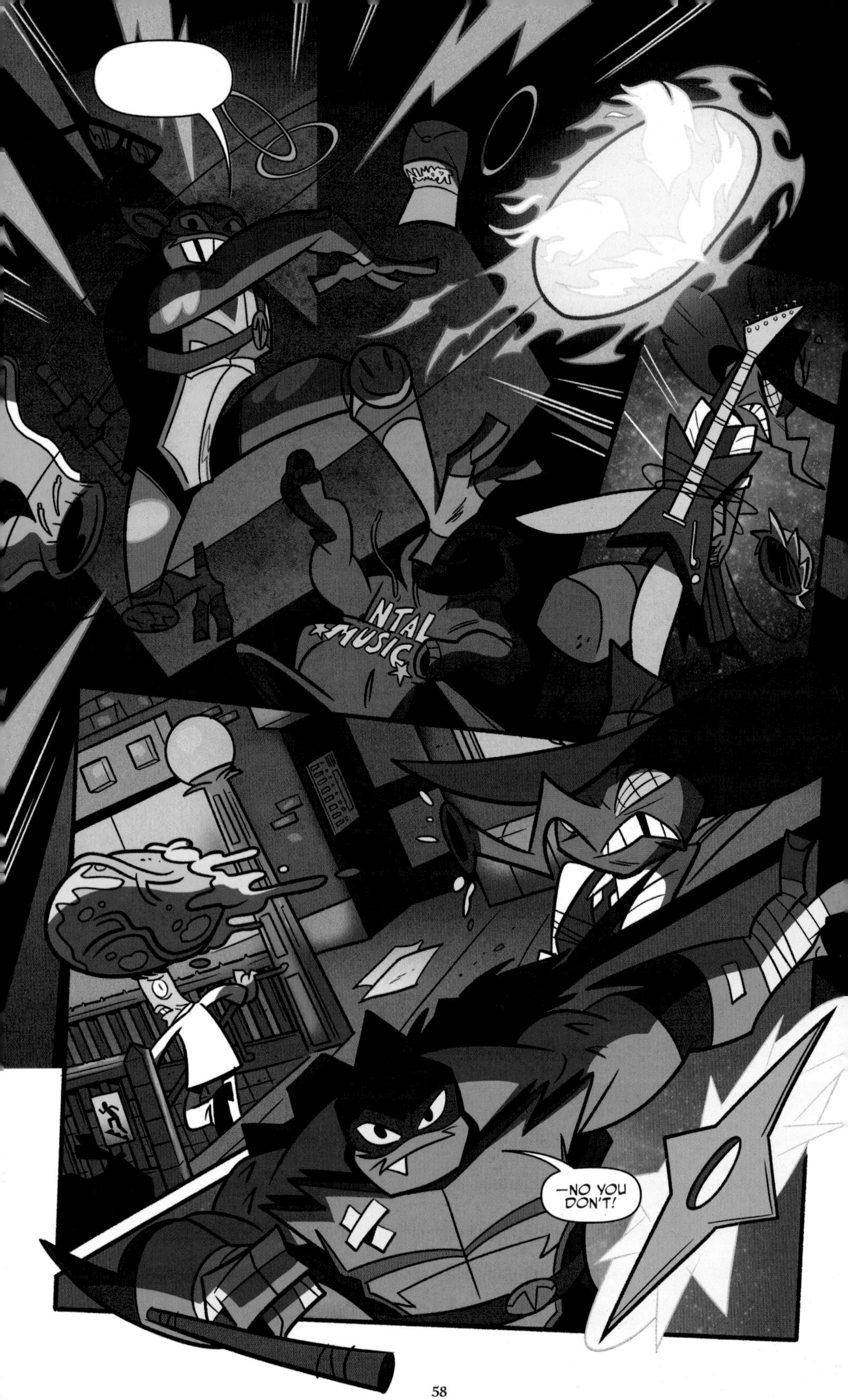
NTAL
MUSIC
—NO YOU DON'T!

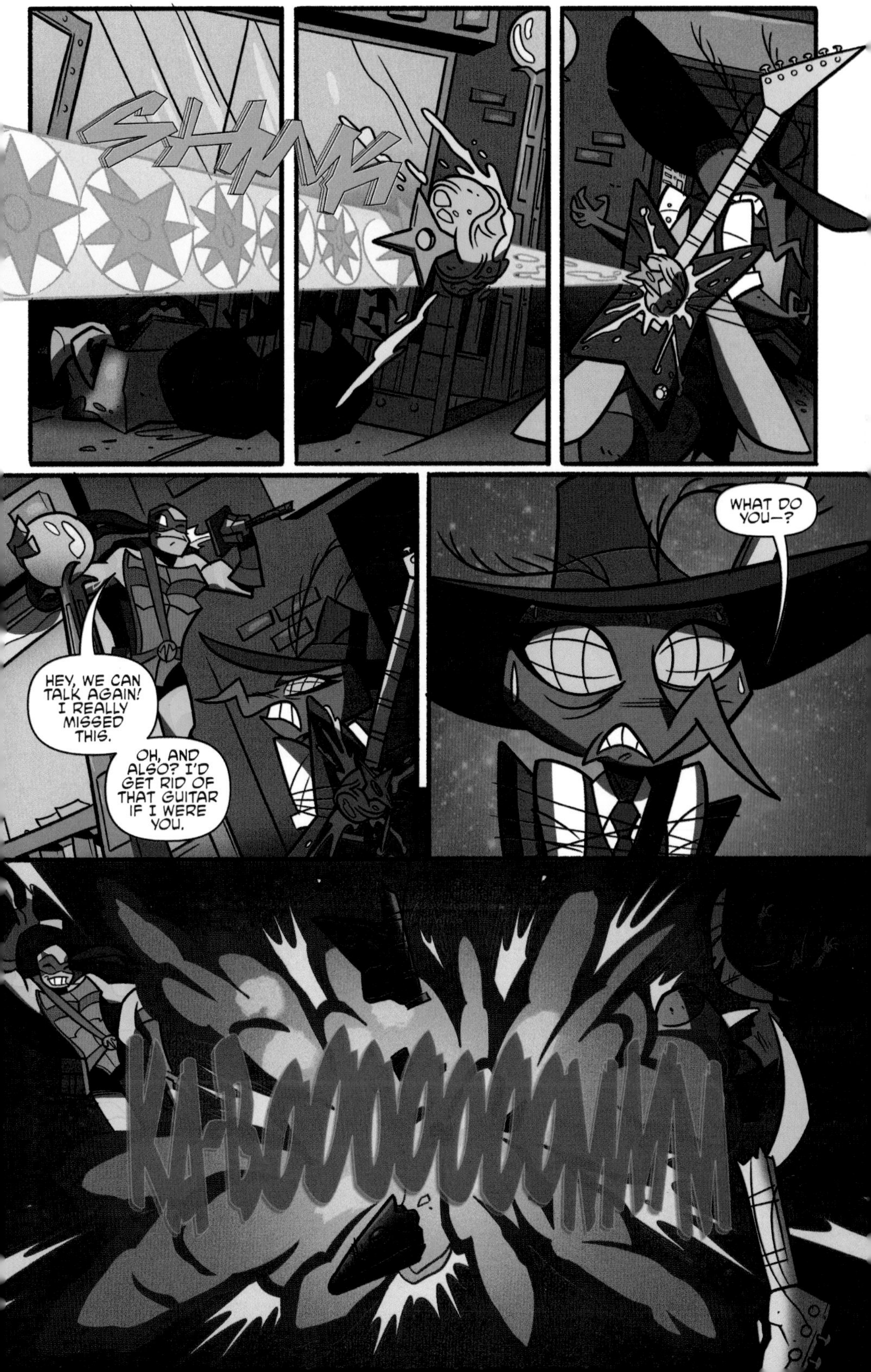
SHUNNK
HEY, WE CAN TALK AGAIN! I REALLY MISSED THIS.
OH, AND ALSO? I'D GET RID OF THAT GUITAR IF I WERE YOU.
WHAT DO YOU—?
KA-BOOOOOOOMMM

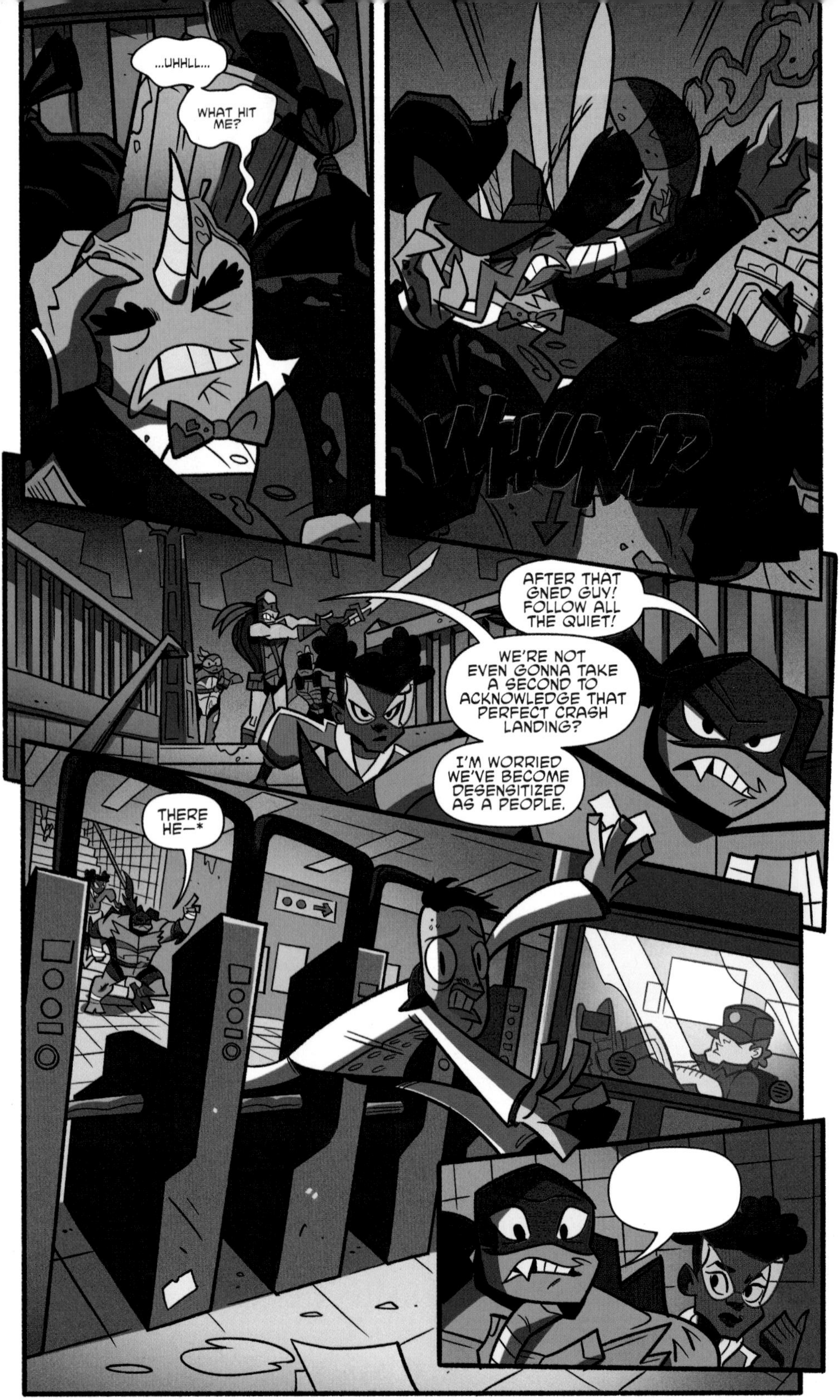
...UHHLL...
WHAT HIT ME?
WHUMP
AFTER THAT GNED GUY! FOLLOW ALL THE QUIET!
WE'RE NOT EVEN GONNA TAKE A SECOND TO ACKNOWLEDGE THAT PERFECT CRASH LANDING?
I'M WORRIED WE'VE BECOME DESENSITIZED AS A PEOPLE.
THERE HE—*

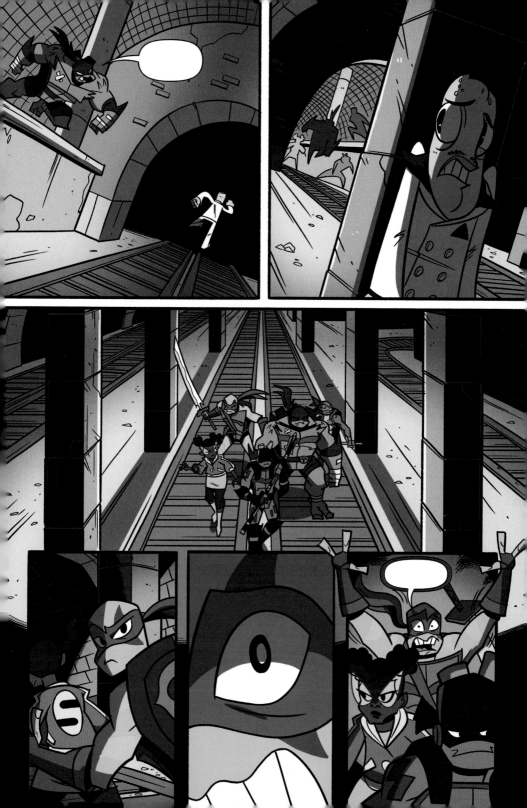

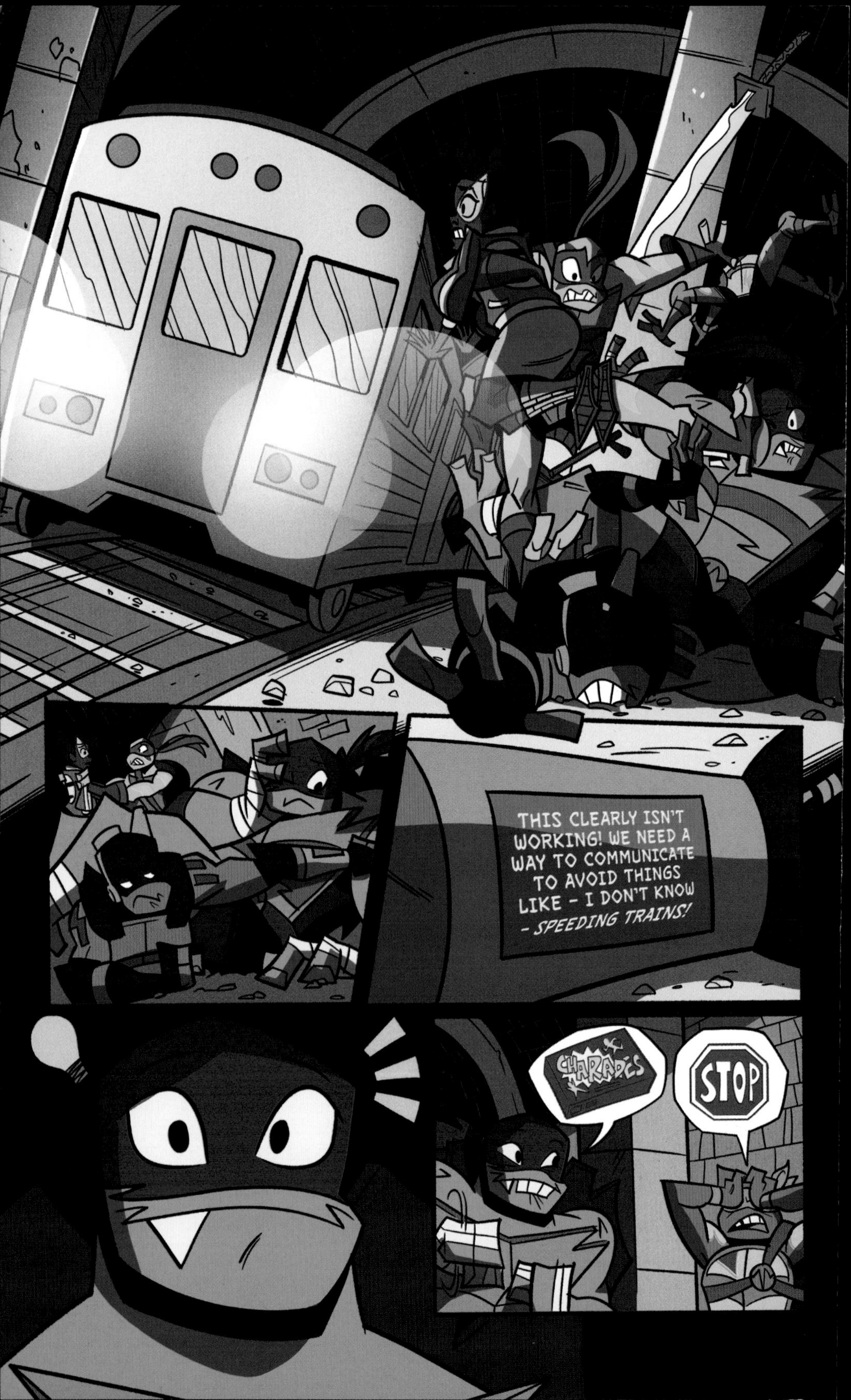

THIS CLEARLY ISN'T WORKING! WE NEED A WAY TO COMMUNICATE TO AVOID THINGS LIKE – I DON'T KNOW – *SPEEDING TRAINS!*
CHARADES
STOP

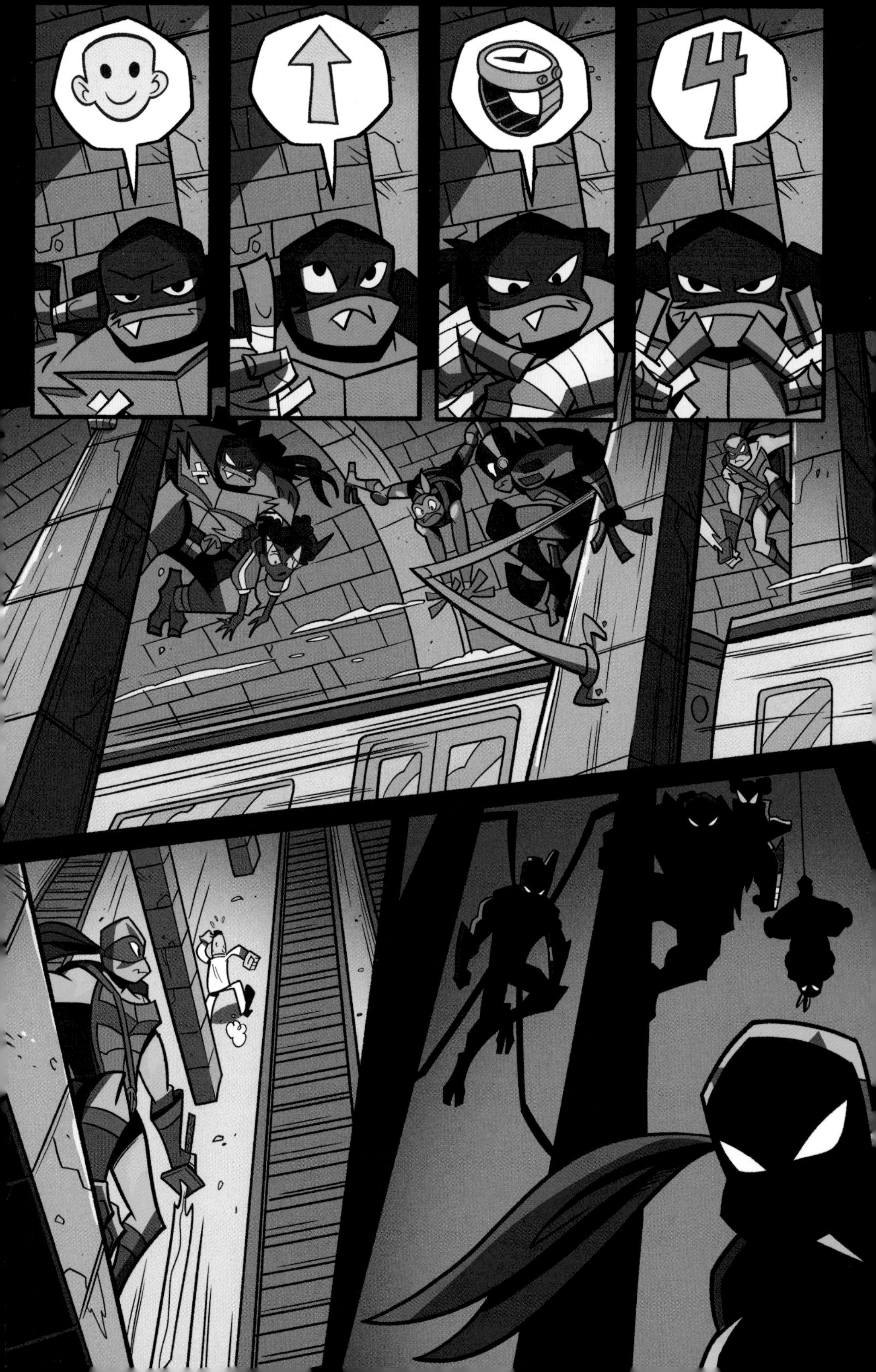
4

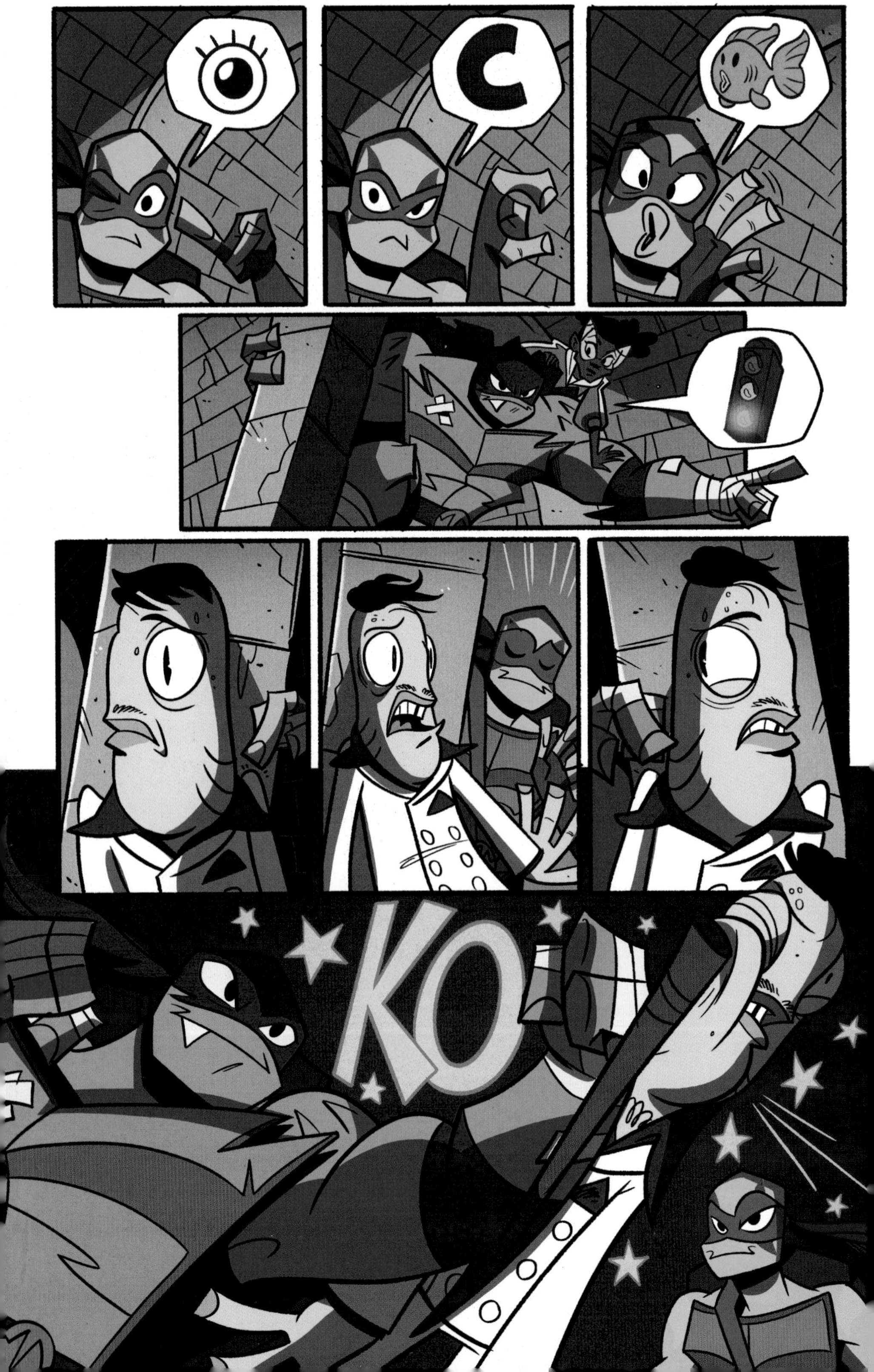
KO

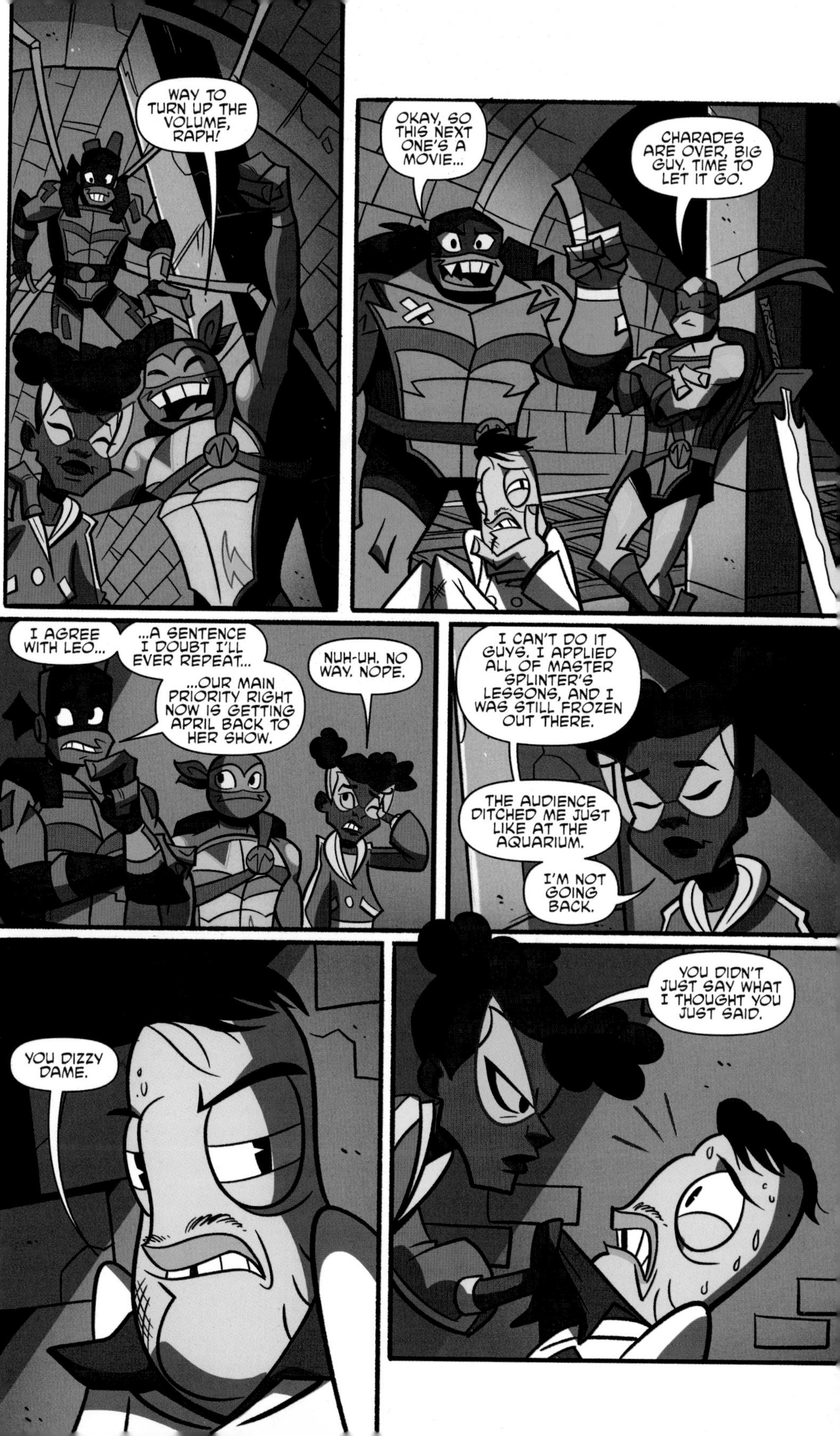
WAY TO TURN UP THE VOLUME, RAPH!
OKAY, SO THIS NEXT ONE'S A MOVIE...
CHARADES ARE OVER, BIG GUY. TIME TO LET IT GO.
I AGREE WITH LEO...
...A SENTENCE I DOUBT I'LL EVER REPEAT...
...OUR MAIN PRIORITY RIGHT NOW IS GETTING APRIL BACK TO HER SHOW.
NUH-UH. NO WAY. NOPE.
I CAN'T DO IT GUYS. I APPLIED ALL OF MASTER SPLINTER'S LESSONS, AND I WAS STILL FROZEN OUT THERE.
THE AUDIENCE DITCHED ME JUST LIKE AT THE AQUARIUM.
I'M NOT GOING BACK.
YOU DIZZY DAME.
YOU DIDN'T JUST SAY WHAT I THOUGHT YOU JUST SAID.

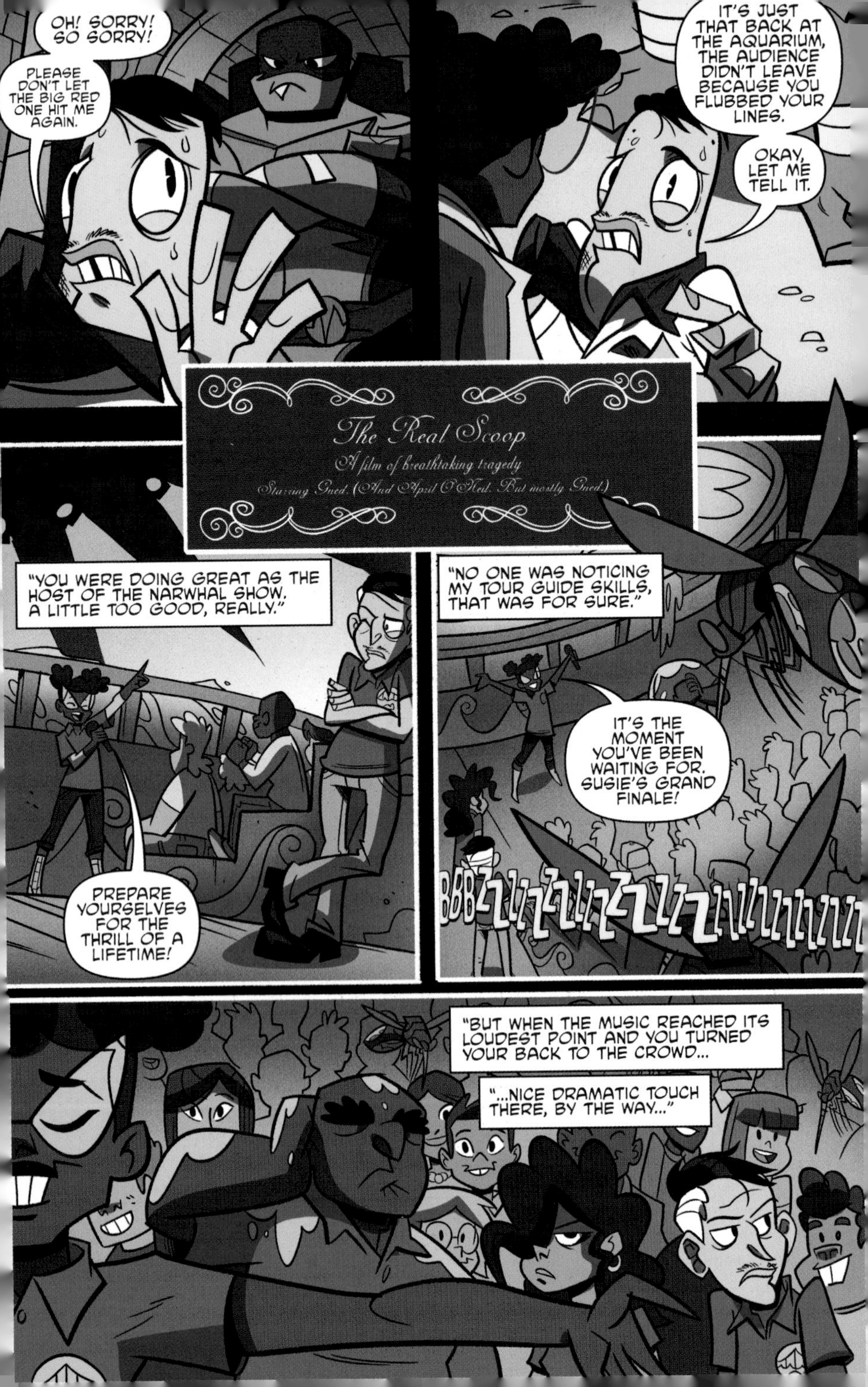
OH! SORRY! SO SORRY!
PLEASE DON'T LET THE BIG RED ONE HIT ME AGAIN.
IT'S JUST THAT BACK AT THE AQUARIUM, THE AUDIENCE DIDN'T LEAVE BECAUSE YOU FLUBBED YOUR LINES.
OKAY, LET ME TELL IT.
The Real Scoop
A film of breathtaking tragedy
Starring Gned. (And April O'Neil. But mostly Gned.)
"YOU WERE DOING GREAT AS THE HOST OF THE NARWHAL SHOW. A LITTLE TOO GOOD, REALLY."
PREPARE YOURSELVES FOR THE THRILL OF A LIFETIME!
"NO ONE WAS NOTICING MY TOUR GUIDE SKILLS, THAT WAS FOR SURE."
IT'S THE MOMENT YOU'VE BEEN WAITING FOR. SUSIE'S GRAND FINALE!
BBBZZZZZZZZZZZZZZZZZZZZZZZZZZZZZZZ
"BUT WHEN THE MUSIC REACHED ITS LOUDEST POINT AND YOU TURNED YOUR BACK TO THE CROWD...
"...NICE DRAMATIC TOUCH THERE, BY THE WAY..."

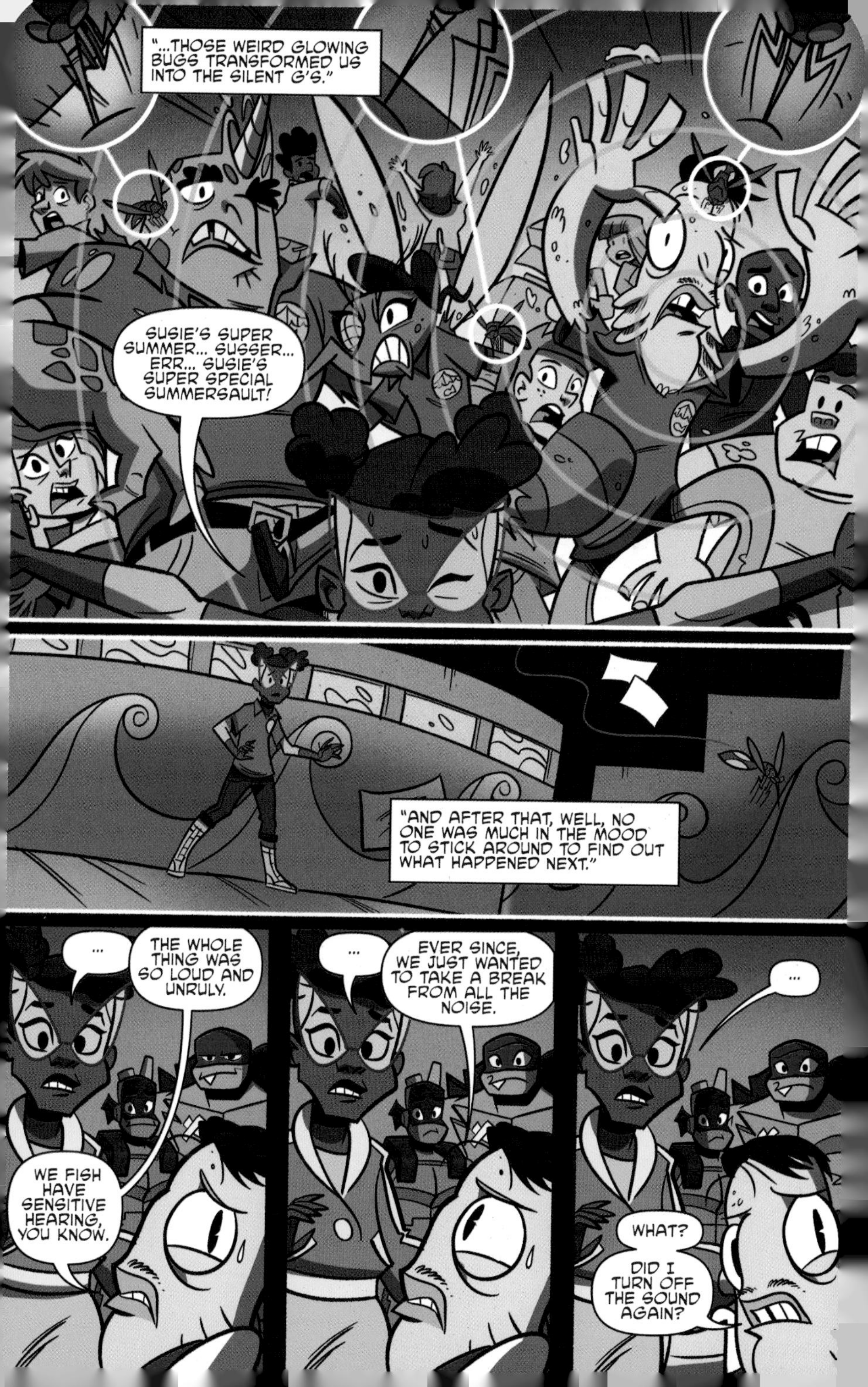
"...THOSE WEIRD GLOWING BUGS TRANSFORMED US INTO THE SILENT G'S."
SUSIE'S SUPER SUMMER... SUSSER... ERR... SUSIE'S SUPER SPECIAL SUMMERSAULT!
"AND AFTER THAT, WELL, NO ONE WAS MUCH IN THE MOOD TO STICK AROUND TO FIND OUT WHAT HAPPENED NEXT."
...
THE WHOLE THING WAS SO LOUD AND UNRULY.
WE FISH HAVE SENSITIVE HEARING, YOU KNOW.
...
EVER SINCE, WE JUST WANTED TO TAKE A BREAK FROM ALL THE NOISE.
...
WHAT?
DID I TURN OFF THE SOUND AGAIN?

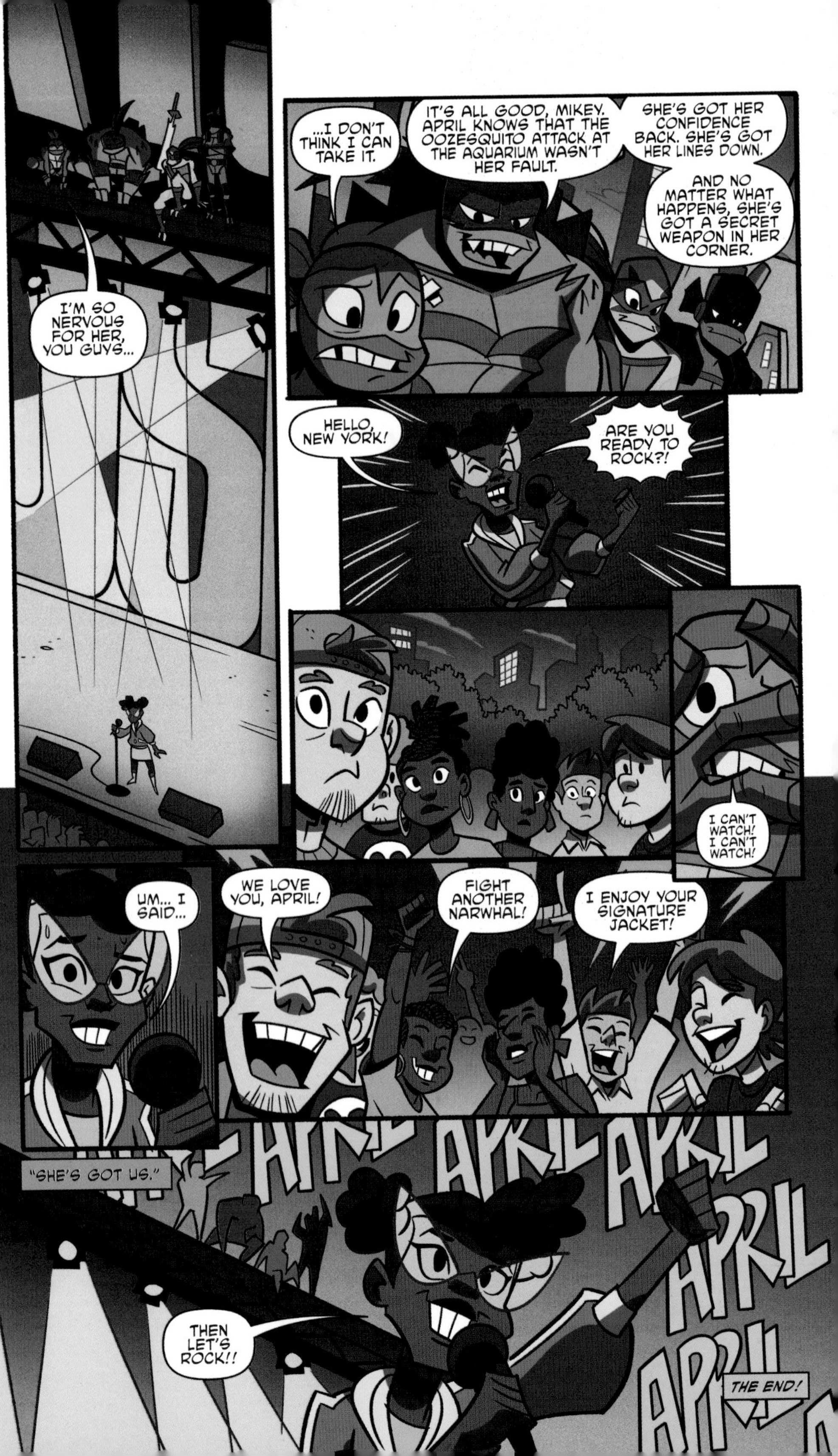
I'M SO NERVOUS FOR HER, YOU GUYS...
...I DON'T THINK I CAN TAKE IT.
IT'S ALL GOOD, MIKEY. APRIL KNOWS THAT THE OOZESQUITO ATTACK AT THE AQUARIUM WASN'T HER FAULT.
SHE'S GOT HER CONFIDENCE BACK. SHE'S GOT HER LINES DOWN.
AND NO MATTER WHAT HAPPENS, SHE'S GOT A SECRET WEAPON IN HER CORNER.
HELLO, NEW YORK!
ARE YOU READY TO ROCK?!
I CAN'T WATCH! I CAN'T WATCH!
UM... I SAID...
WE LOVE YOU, APRIL!
FIGHT ANOTHER NARWHAL!
I ENJOY YOUR SIGNATURE JACKET!
"SHE'S GOT US."
APRIL APRIL APRIL APRIL
THEN LET'S ROCK!!
THE END!

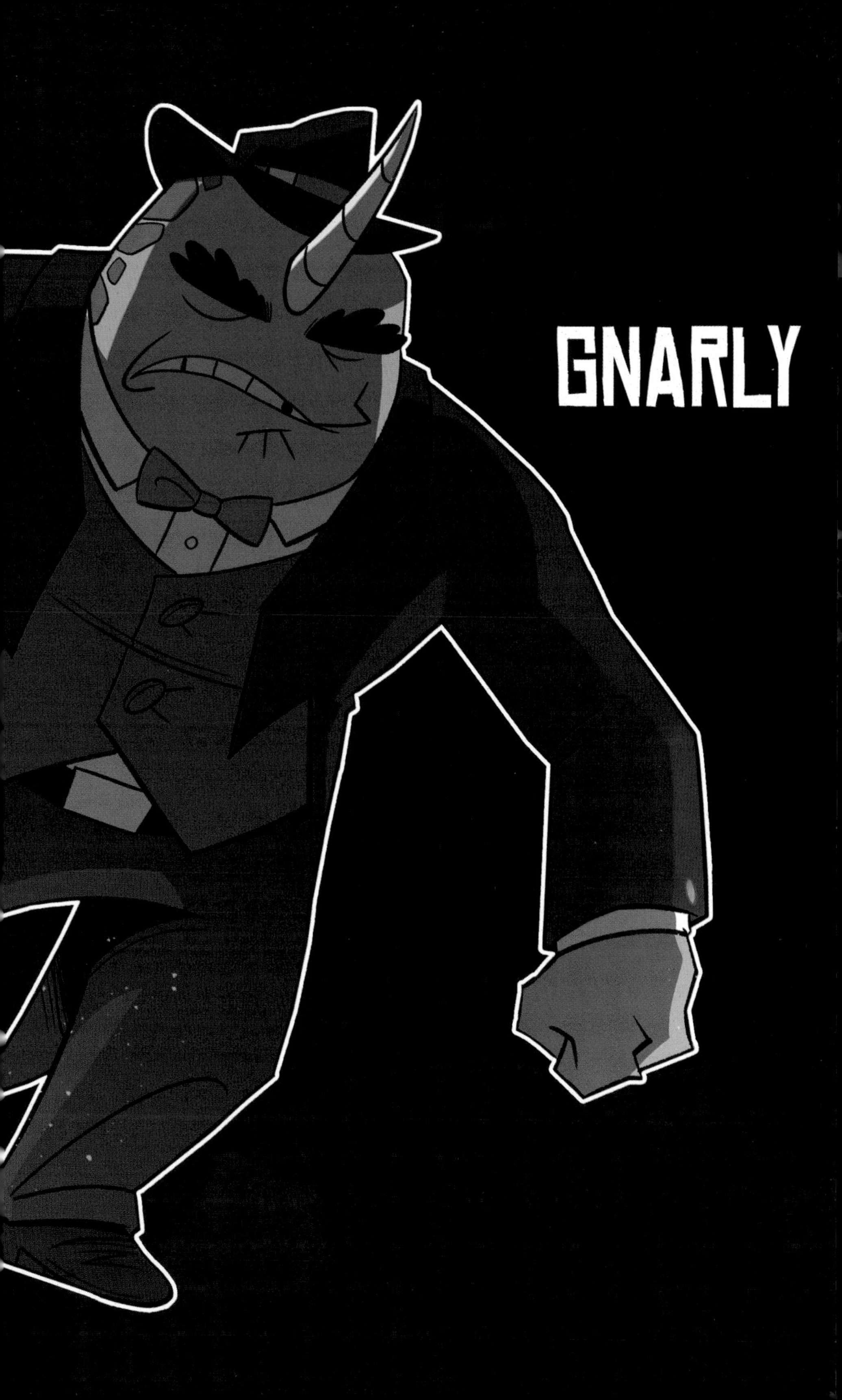
GNARLY

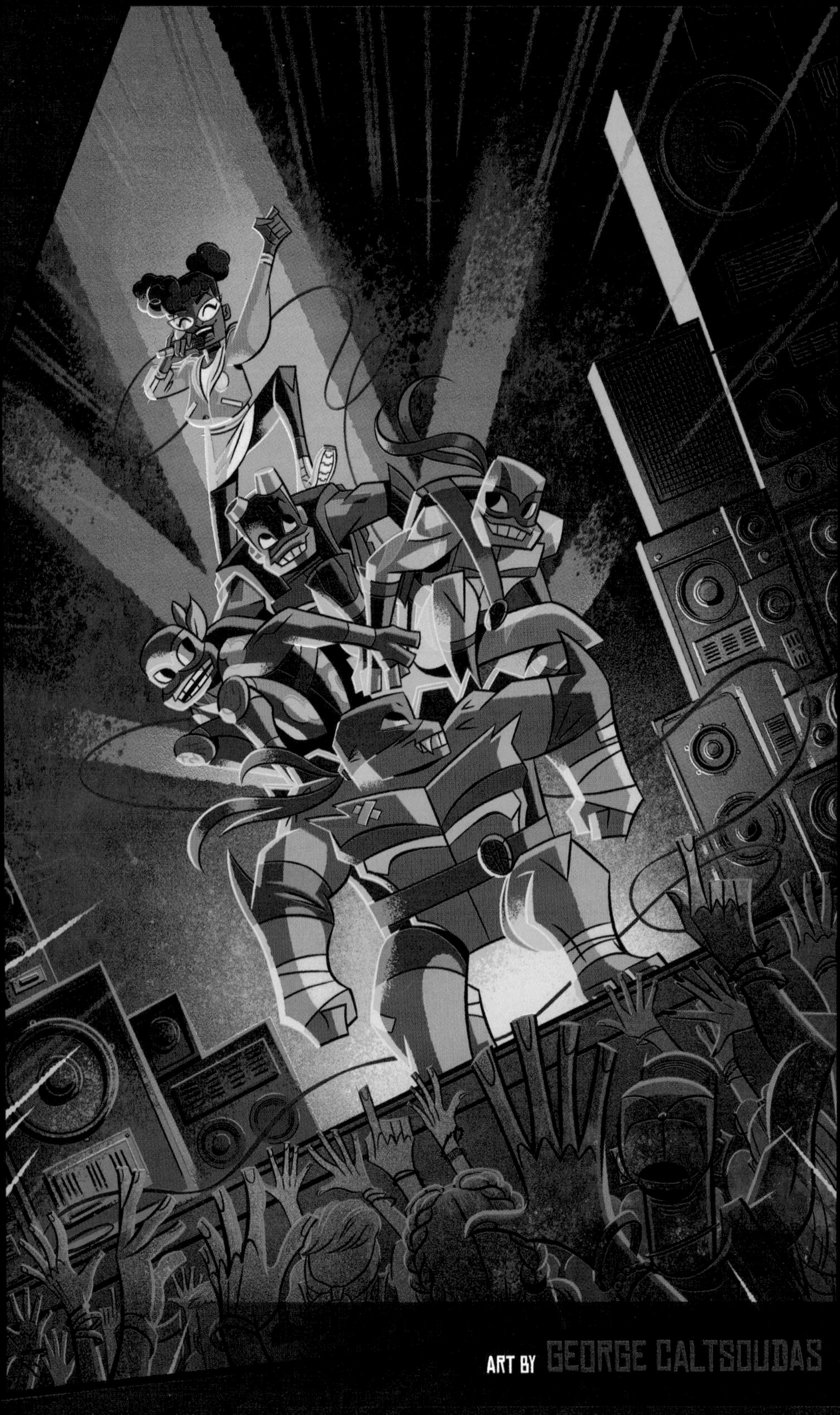

ART BY GEORGE CALTSOUDAS

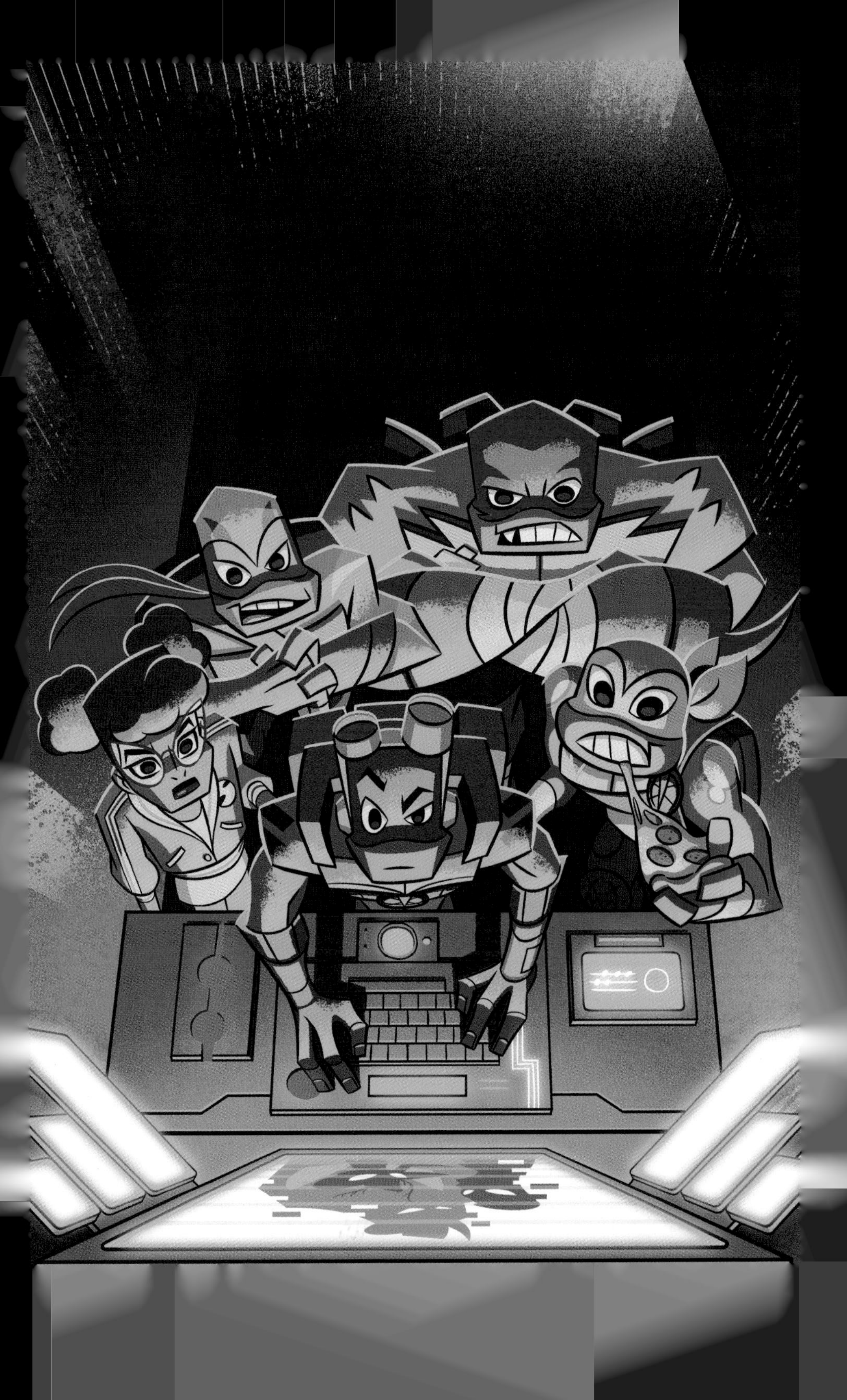

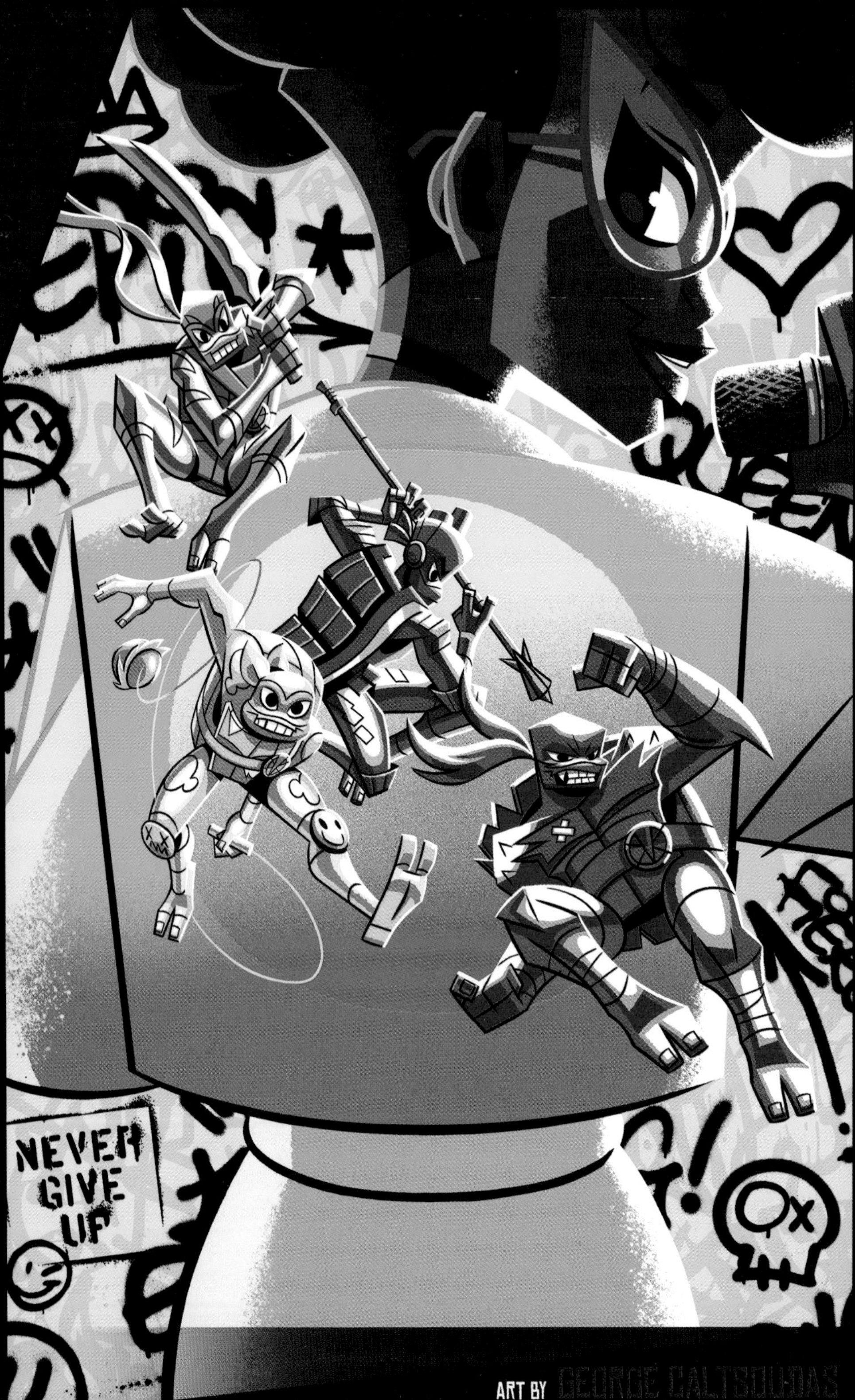
NEVER GIVE UP

ART BY GEORGE CALTSOUDAS